Connie ~
Happy
Birthday!
Janice Thompson

ELEANOR JO
The Farmer's Daughter

ELEANOR JO

The Farmer's Daughter

ELEANOR CLARK

HONOR NET

THE HONOR NETWORK

Dedication

O MY GRANDCHILDREN AND GREAT grandchildren. May you recognize, love, and appreciate your rich Christian heritage and the privilege of living in America, which was founded on the trust and hope we have in Jesus. May you continue the legacy.

Contents

*T*O MY LORD AND SAVIOR, JESUS CHRIST, who has blessed me with the greatest family, life, and country. May every word bring honor and glory to Your name.

To my publisher, Jake Jones, who recognized the potential of my stories and my heart's desire to bless and encourage young readers to value their American and Christian heritage.

To my writer, Janice Thompson, who understood my love of history and breathed life into my stories with the skill of her pen.

To Annabelle Meyers who helped develop the character lessons.

Be ye strong therefore, and let not your hands be weak: for your work shall be rewarded.

— 2 Chronicles 15:7

"You're working really hard as a freshman, and then you've got all of your basketball games, besides. I'm really proud of you for all you're trying to accomplish, and that's why I've brought you here today."

KEEP YOUR EYE
ON THE GOAL

*R*ACHEL ANN RAN FROM ONE END OF THE basketball court to the other, careful not to lose the ball to her opponents. The score was tied, and only a few seconds remained in the game. The cheers from the crowd made her want to win the game even more. Out of the corner of her eye, well above the heads of the other players, she spied the goal. Could she make the shot from here? The fourteen-year-old bent her knees, dribbled the ball, and quickly released it into the air. She loved the way it felt as it lifted from her fingertips and the whooshing sound it made as it flew through the air.

Just before the final buzzer sounded, the basketball dropped through the hoop, and the people in the crowd went wild. The shouts of joy were deafening. Was it possible? Had she really led the Jaguars to victory in the final game of the season—right here, in her own high school gymnasium? Joy washed over her, and for a moment, she felt like she would cry. Still, there was no time for that now.

Rachel Ann's teammates swarmed around her, giving her high fives and warm hugs. Their laughter and smiles were contagious. Off in the distance, she saw the grin on her coach's face, his arms raised in victory. Finally, when she was able to focus, Rachel Ann looked up into the stands, trying to locate her family. There! She saw her mother and her grandmother too. They were on their feet, cheering. She waved, and her grandmother, the one she lovingly called Grand Doll, waved a gold and black pennant in the air. Rachel Ann couldn't help but chuckle. Her grandmother was her biggest fan.

Moments later, she found herself on the podium, receiving the MVP (Most Valuable Player) award. She could hardly believe it. Nothing could have prepared her for such a thing. Her heart beat so hard and fast, she thought it would never calm down. Had all of her hard work this year really paid off? What a wonderful way to end the season.

As soon as the awards ceremony ended, her mom and Grand Doll rushed to meet her.

"I'm so proud of you, honey," her mother said, wrapping her in a tight embrace.

"You're the best one out there by far," Grand Doll added, giving her a kiss on the cheek. "In fact, I don't know when I've ever seen a better player."

Rachel Ann giggled. Surely Grand Doll exaggerated, but Rachel Ann didn't mind. It made her feel good to know she had led the basketball team to victory. In fact, many things about her first year in high school felt good: making the team, being named Christian athlete of the year, and making good grades. All of it. Still, it was enough to make her really tired, and she felt worn out at times. She always seemed to be busy. After school, she had basketball practice and then all of her homework. Add to that her chores at home, and she hardly had any free time at all.

Some days, she just wanted to stay home in bed and pull the covers over her head and sleep, but there was always more work to do. Rachel Ann stifled a yawn as she thought about it.

"Ready to go?" her mom asked.

"Mmm-hmm," Rachel Ann nodded. "Just let me change and I'll be right back out."

She took a quick shower in the locker room and then quickly dressed in her jeans and a pink T-shirt. After pulling her hair back in a ponytail, she slipped on a pair of tennis shoes. Finally, knowing it was chilly outside, she reached for her jacket.

As she walked out of the locker room, her mother and grandmother came up to meet her. "Grand Doll is going to take you for a special treat, honey. I will see you at home later," her mother said with a smile. Then she gave her daughter another big hug and exclaimed, "I am so proud of you!"

A few minutes later, Rachel Ann was seated in Grand Doll's car. As they pulled away from the school, her grandmother set out on a different road than expected. Rachel Ann looked around, confused. "Where are we going?" she asked.

"I thought you might like some ice cream to celebrate your victory!" Grand Doll announced. "I know it's you're favorite. It's mine too."

"Mmm! Thanks!" Even though it was cold outside, ice cream sounded terrific to Rachel Ann.

A short time later, they stopped at an ice cream shop and ordered their favorite ice cream. Rachel Ann ordered a double-dip of rocky road in a waffle cone, and Grand Doll ordered a dish of pralines 'n cream. Rachel Ann shivered as she ate but didn't mind a bit. She would eat ice cream every day if she could!

As Rachel Ann nibbled away, Grand Doll kept talking about how proud she was of Rachel Ann's performance. On and on Grand Doll went. Rachel Ann just smiled— inside and out.

After they had finished their ice cream, they climbed back into the car. Rachel Ann leaned her head back against the seat and closed her eyes. She replayed the afternoon's events one by one: taking the final shot, looking up at the scoreboard, listening to the cheers, and standing on the podium.

As she thought back over these things, she grew quite sleepy. Before she knew it, she was fast asleep. She dreamed of dribbling the ball and of hearing the crowd yell, "Jaguars! Jaguars! Jaguars!"

Only when the car hit some bumps in the road and started to stop did Rachel Ann awaken. Realizing they weren't at her house, she sat up and looked out the window. They seemed to be someplace out in the country. Through the glare of the bright afternoon sun shining down, she could barely make out a house on the far end of the property. It looked strangely familiar.

Off to the right and left were acres and acres of land. Trees dotted the landscape, their branches bare and dry. In the distance, beyond the fence, Rachel Ann saw several horses and some cows. The whole thing was very pretty, but she wasn't sure why they had stopped.

"Where are we, Grand Doll?"

Her grandmother looked back in her direction as she explained. "This is my childhood home where I lived as a little girl."

"Wow! Are you serious?" Rachel Ann peered out of the window in earnest at the tiny wood-framed house. Though she had often heard about the dairy farm where Grand Doll was raised, she hadn't been here in years.

I just love coming back to the little town of Mexia, Texas, where I grew up."

"Why do you call it Me-*he*-a?" Rachel asked, trying to push back another yawn. "Isn't it spelled M-e-x-i-a?"

Grand Doll chuckled. "I asked that same question dozens of times when I was young. The Spanish pronunciation of the word is Me-*he*-a, trust me! The town was named for General Mexia's family, who lived here in the 1830s."

"Wow. What was it like to grow up in such a small place, so far from the big city?" Rachel Ann asked.

"It didn't feel small to me as a young girl. In fact, Mexia seemed large to me! It was a wonderful place, filled with kind-hearted people, quaint shops, close-knit churches, and folks with hopes and dreams—just like you!"

"Really?" Rachel Ann shrugged. She still couldn't imagine it.

"Some of my growing up years took place during the Great Depression," her grandmother explained. "Do you remember hearing about that?"

"Wasn't the Depression in the 1930s?" Rachel Ann asked.

"That's right," Grand Doll nodded.

"I know a little about it," Rachel Ann said. "My history teacher told us it was a hard time for people all across the country. Many were out of work, and others lived very poorly."

"Yes. Thankfully, my papa had plenty of work—the dairy farm kept him busy. But life was still very hard at times. We didn't always have money for clothes and shoes. Still, my mama grew vegetables in the garden, so there was always plenty to eat."

"Sounds like a hard life, Grand Doll."

"Why, no need to feel sorry for me," her grandmother said with a smile. "We didn't feel deprived at all. We had a good life, a blessed life. Perhaps we didn't have a lot of things, but we had each other."

"I guess things were really different back then," Rachel said with another shrug. She couldn't imagine growing her own food or doing without shoes.

"Oh, very!" Grand Doll exclaimed. "Life was different in hundreds of ways. Remember, back in those days there was no such thing as the Internet or even computers."

"No way!"

"Way!" Her grandmother gave a hearty laugh. "For that matter, there was no television. No video games either."

Rachel Ann's eyes grew wide and she looked at her grandmother in amazement. "That's hard to imagine. What did you do for fun?"

Grand doll laughed.

"We did what all children did," Grand Doll explained. "We worked hard on the farm, gathering eggs, tending to the chores, shelling peas, shucking corn, and caring for the animals. Then, when the work was done, we played with our brothers, sisters, and friends. Much of the time, we made up our own games, but there were always plenty of children around, and the games were always fun. We worked our way toward the goal, just like you did today."

"Wow!"

"I lived on this dairy farm as a youngster and worked alongside my papa every morning before school. It was a hard life, but a good one, as I said."

"Wow. I thought *my* schedule was tough," Rachel said with a sigh.

"I know that you are going through a tough time right now, honey," Grand Doll said. "You're working really hard as a freshman, and then you've got all of your basketball games, besides. I'm really proud of you for all you're trying to accomplish, and that's why I've brought you here today."

"Really?" It made Rachel Ann happy to know her grandmother was proud of her.

"Really," Grand Doll replied. "The Bible says in 2 Chronicles 15:7, *Be ye strong therefore, and let not your hands be weak: for your work shall be rewarded.*"

"I've heard my mom quote that verse many times," Rachel Ann said.

"People in our family have always been hard workers," Grand Doll said with a nod. "I remember my parents were always working, throughout the Depression, and even after, when the war came."

"War?" Rachel Ann's eyes grew big. "There was a war? Here? In Mexia?"

Her grandmother shook her head, and as she did, a faraway look came into her eyes. "No, the war I'm referring to was World War II, and it took place overseas in Europe and beyond. But it affected us here in Mexia when I was a little younger than you."

"Wow," Rachel Ann said.

"Would you like me to tell you the story?"

"Oh, yes ma'am." She wanted to hear it, for sure.

Her grandmother's eyes sparkled merrily as they always did when she was about to share a great story. "Well then, come with me child, and I'll tell you all about it."

Together, they climbed out of the car and made their way up the long, narrow driveway. When they drew close to the small farmhouse, Grand Doll stopped, and with a twinkle in her eye, she turned to look at Rachel Ann.

"It all started right here," she said with a wink. "Right in this very spot, in fact."

And so the amazing story of Eleanor Jo began…

"Good morning, little hens!" Eleanor Jo said, moving quickly from nest to nest, filling her tiny basket with the delicate, golden-colored eggs.

LIFE ON THE FARM

MEXIA, TEXAS
FRIDAY, DECEMBER 5, 1941

*T*EN-YEAR-OLD ELEANOR JO BUNDLED UP in her winter coat and ran out of the back door to begin her morning chores. Her honey-brown braids bounced against her shoulders as she skipped along. In her hand, she clutched a small woven basket. Off in the distance, the morning sun rose against the eastern sky, casting a pinkish glow over the dairy farm where she had lived most of her young life. She loved this time of day best of all, when everything was quiet and still. She loved this farm so much. Surely, it was the prettiest place in all the world.

She looked up at the winter skies, heavy with clouds, and shivered. Then she headed off to the henhouse to gather freshly-laid eggs, just as she did every morning at about this same time. Once she stepped inside the small shed, the hens began to cluck and scurry about on the dirt floor, searching for bits of food.

"Good morning, little hens!" Eleanor Jo said, moving quickly from nest to nest, filling her tiny basket with the delicate, golden-colored eggs. She was careful to avoid the nests with hens sitting on them, for fear of getting the back of her hand pecked. How many times had those critters nibbled at her hands? Dozens!

All along the way, she chatted with the hens, thanking them for laying such beautiful, large brown eggs. "If not for you, we would have nothing to eat in the mornings!" she said with a giggle. They responded by clucking loudly.

Just when she finished her task, the door to the henhouse swung open and her younger brother James entered. As he did, a blast of cold air blew in.

"It's fr…freezing out there!" the six-year-old said with chattering teeth.

"What are you doing in here?" Eleanor Jo scolded in her most grownup voice. "Why aren't you fetching wood for the pot-bellied stove so that Mama can start breakfast for the family?"

"I've already done that," he explained. "Besides, Mama sent me here to find you. She says you should hurry this morning because Papa has to work in the oil fields after he milks the cows and feeds the hogs. He's going to be mighty hungry."

Eleanor Jo pushed a loose piece of hair out of her face and nodded. "I'm nearly done."

She finished filling her little basket in a hurry and then closed the door of the henhouse tightly so that the wild animals wouldn't find their way inside. A little shiver ran down her spine as she remembered the day, a few years before, when Mama had forgotten to close the door and a coyote had gotten inside. What a terrible day that had been! They'd lost many of their best laying hens.

Eleanor Jo pushed the awful memory away and quickly headed back toward the house, careful not to spill the eggs as she ran. In her younger years, she had accidentally dropped the eggs many times. But now that she was ten, she hardly ever broke the eggs anymore. The older she had grown, the more responsible she had become.

Eleanor Jo liked being responsible. In fact, she liked most everything about growing up, especially the part where her papa's friends smiled and said, "You are your father's daughter!" Oh, how she loved that! Her papa was a hard worker, and she wanted to be just like him.

She entered the house through the back door and smiled as she saw Mama pulling biscuits out of the oven. Their wonderful scent filled the tiny kitchen and made

Eleanor Jo's mouth water. She could hardly wait for breakfast!

"There you are, Eleanor Jo!" her mother said with a smile. "I'll take those eggs off your hands now. Papa should be finishing up his chores soon, and I'm running behind this morning."

"Yes ma'am. Do you need me to pump the water this morning?" Eleanor Jo asked as she turned back toward the door in preparation for the task. Pumping water in the springhouse was always her chore.

But Mama surprised her when she said, "Not this morning, darling. Your sister took care of that for you today."

"Really? How wonderful!"

As Mama prepared breakfast, Eleanor Jo scrambled out of her coat and went in search of her younger sister, Martha Ann, to thank her. She found the eight-year-old in the bedroom, fussing with her hair.

"Do you need help with your ribbon?" Eleanor Jo asked.

Martha Ann turned with a pout. "Yes, please."

Eleanor Jo smiled as she tied the white ribbon at the top of her sister's head and then stared at Martha Ann's beautiful curls. "There. You will be the prettiest girl in school today."

"No, *you're* the pretty one!" Martha Ann insisted.

"Me?" Eleanor Jo turned to look at herself in the mirror. Her big brown eyes were her nicest feature, she supposed. At least, that's what Mama always said. And, even though it was mid-winter, her hair still carried a bit of the shimmer from last summer's days in the sun. Still, she'd never really thought of herself as pretty, though it made her feel good to hear Martha Ann say so.

"I want to be just like you when I grow up," her younger sister said with a sigh. "You're so talented and so smart."

"I am?"

"Yes! You can play baseball just like the boys, and you play the piano so well. You're the teacher's pet too."

"Me? Teacher's pet?" Eleanor Jo pretended she didn't know what her sister was talking about, but she couldn't help but smile. She enjoyed being a good student, and she loved to play baseball too. In many ways, Martha Ann was right. There were a great many things Eleanor Jo was good at, though she hated to brag.

She gave herself one last look in the mirror, then she grabbed her sister by the hand, and they skipped into the kitchen together. Just then, Papa came in through the back door, singing a happy song. He always sounded happy in the mornings, especially on days when he woke them up with his morning song:

Wake up and spit on the rock. It ain't quite day, but it's
   four o'clock.
I know you're tired and sleepy too, but honey, we've got
   work to do!

Somehow, just hearing that song every morning made getting up a little easier. Right now, though, he wasn't singing the morning song. He was singing one of his favorite hymns "It Is Well with My Soul." His voice rang out:

"When peace like a river attendeth my way
And sorrows like sea billows roll
Whatever my lot, Thou hast taught me to say
'It is well, it is well with my soul.'"

Eleanor Jo loved that song and joined right in. Oh, how she loved to sing!

When the song ended, the whole family gathered around the table. After Papa blessed the food, they began to eat. The baking powder biscuits were light, golden, and fluffy, as always, and the fresh scrambled eggs were delicious. After the meal, Papa took a sip from his steaming cup of coffee and leaned back in his chair, smiling at Mama, who looked as regal as a queen with her dark curls and starched white dress.

"You've done it again, darling," he said. "You made a breakfast fit for a king!"

Her mother's cheeks turned pink as she answered, "Why, thank you."

"What are your plans for the day?" Papa asked her.

"I will spend the morning canning," Mama explained. "Then, after the girls come home from school, they can help me prepare a special dinner. I'm planning to slice up some of that wonderful smoked ham and roast corn on the cob."

"Mmm, my favorite!" James said. "I love corn on the cob."

Eleanor Jo couldn't help but agree with her little brother. In fact, she loved most of the foods that Mama cooked, especially the vegetables fresh from the garden. One day she would be a good cook just like her mother. That's what Papa always said, anyway.

"We have a very good life, don't we?" Papa said with a grin.

"Yes!" they all chimed in.

Eleanor Jo couldn't think of a better life, in fact. To be here on the farm with her parents and her brother and sister, to live in a town where they knew their neighbors and worshiped in a wonderful church—what more could anyone ask for?

Just then, Mama clapped her hands, getting every-one's attention. "Better hurry, children," she said. "You don't want to miss the school bus. Bundle up! It's cold outside."

Eleanor Jo and her brother and sister scrambled into their winter coats and gave their parents goodbye kisses. Then they headed out the back door and down the long driveway toward the road that led to town. Once they reached the edge of the road, they stood there, waiting for the school bus, shivering all the while.

Eleanor Jo looked back toward the house with a smile on her face. As much as she loved going to school, she could hardly wait to return home again to help Mama with supper. There was just something about this wonderful place that always made her happy…from the inside out.

---

*That meant she—Eleanor Jo—was
the only child in the family who
understood what a sad day this was.*

NEWS OF WAR

DECEMBER 7, 1941

THE FOLLOWING SUNDAY, ELEANOR JO and her family returned home from church and ate a wonderful dinner together. Then it was time for their Sunday rest. Shortly after drifting off to sleep, Eleanor Jo awoke to the sound of crying. She quickly made her way to the living room, where she found Mama and Papa seated in front of the big radio. Tears were streaming down Mama's face, and Papa paced back and forth with a worried look as he listened to the man on the radio. The fellow had a booming voice, and he sounded very serious. Eleanor Jo tried to make sense of his words, but she couldn't figure out what he was talking about.

"What is it, Papa?" she asked. "What has happened?"

Her father shook his head and put a finger to his lips to let her know she needed to wait to ask her questions until after he listened a little longer. She tried really hard to be still and quiet for as long as she could, but after a few minutes, she grew restless.

"Please tell me, Mama," she finally whispered.

Something bad had happened. She could tell from the tears in her mother's eyes and the wrinkles on her papa's brow.

Mama stood and motioned for Eleanor Jo to follow her out to the hallway, where she began to explain. "President Roosevelt is speaking to the American people today because something very tragic has happened this morning." She gave Eleanor Jo a serious look as she asked, "Do you know about the war that's going on—on the other side of the world?"

"Oh yes," Eleanor Jo said with a nod. Her teacher, Mrs. Evans, had told the class all about it—about an evil man from Germany named Hitler who was mistreating people and who wanted to take over all of Europe. The Italians and Japanese were fighting to take control of many other countries as well.

A little shiver ran down her spine as she thought about it. At least, thank goodness, there was no threat of war here…in America.

"Something has happened this very morning," her mother said. Tears began to trickle down her cheeks.

"What, Mama?"

"The Japanese have bombed American troops at Pearl Harbor."

"Pearl Harbor? Where is that?" Surely it was a long way from here, but how terrible to know that American men had been attacked!

Mama went on to explain that several thousand American servicemen were stationed on ships at a place called Pearl Harbor in Hawaii. Many of those men, she said, had lost their lives that very morning when the Japanese dropped bombs on their ships, and many others had been injured as well. Mama began to weep again, clutching her hands at her chest. "When I think of those young men, it just breaks my heart."

Eleanor Jo started to pace up and down the hallway, just like she'd seen Papa do in the living room. She didn't want to cry, but how could she help it? This was terrible news—the worst! *Young soldiers, whose lives had been lost? What would their families do without them?* She could hardly stand to think of such a thing!

Within seconds, tears ran down her cheeks. "What will happen next, Mama?" she tearfully asked.

"I'm not sure," her mother replied as she glanced back toward the living room. Papa now stood directly in front of the radio. "That's why we are listening to the man on the radio."

"But...," Eleanor Jo stammered, "does this mean America will enter the war? Will our boys and our men have to go to Japan and Germany to fight?" What a dreadful thought!

"That decision is in the hands of our president and Congress," Mama said. "We will pray and see what the Lord leads them to do."

Just then, Martha Ann came skipping down the hallway with her rag doll in her arms. Her curls bobbed up and down as she skipped along. She quickly realized something was wrong. "W...what has happened?" she asked, coming to a stop. "Is something wrong with Papa?"

"No, darling," Mama whispered.

"James?"

"No." Mama shook her head. "This has nothing to do with anyone in our family, so rest easy about that. Something else has happened. We will discuss it together later. For now, perhaps it would be best if you children went out into the yard to play while Papa and I have a discussion."

"Aren't we going to church this evening?" Martha Ann asked, sounding shocked. They always went to church on Sunday evening.

"I feel sure we will go," Mama explained. "There will be many who will want to gather together to pray. We will want to be there with them. Just give us a few minutes, girls." With a worried look, she added, "And please keep an eye on your little brother until we leave."

"Of course, Mama," Eleanor Jo said.

Martha Ann plodded along behind Eleanor Jo, down the hall, through the kitchen, and out the back door. They found James playing with Luke and Maggie, their dogs.

"Fetch, Luke!" James tossed a ball, and the happy dog ran after it, snatched it up, and then ran back. As he dropped it at James's feet, his tail wagged happily.

Eleanor Jo watched as her little brother threw the ball again. Her heart grew heavy when she realized the truth of it. He was so young, he had no idea what was going on with the war. Martha Ann certainly didn't know what had happened this morning, either. That meant she—Eleanor Jo—was the only child in the family who understood what a sad day this was. She would have to mourn all alone—until Mama and Papa called them back into the house, anyway.

She sat on the back porch steps and leaned her chin into her hands. Martha Ann sat next to her.

"Can you tell me why everyone is so sad, or must I wait to hear it from Mama and Papa later?" her younger sister whispered. "I'm scared."

"I know you are, Martha Ann," Eleanor Jo said in her most grown-up voice, "but I think Papa will want to tell you, so you must wait."

With a sigh, her sister rose and went off to play with their little brother. Just then, their dog Luke jumped on James. His large paws covered James with mud. "No, Luke, no!" James shouted.

Eleanor Jo stood up and walked over to her brother. "You can't go to church looking like that, now can you?"

He shrugged, and she began to help him brush the dirt off of his pants and shirt. Then Eleanor Jo sat down once again and looked out over the farm. Was it really possible that just two days ago, she and Martha Ann were playing with their school friends, happy and carefree? And now, just two days later, everything had changed?

War.

The very word frightened her. It seemed people and countries were always fighting to steal land that wasn't theirs, but why? It didn't make a bit of sense to her. Stealing was wrong and hurting people was wrong too. For goodness sake! Why couldn't bad men like Hitler just read the Bible and follow God's commands? If only they would decide to obey the Golden Rule—*Do unto others as you would have others do unto you*—then everyone would get along, and there would be no need for fighting. What a wonderful world it would be...just as wonderful as her life here on the farm.

Her teacher, Mrs. Evans, always said that the children should pray for their leaders, and Eleanor Jo prayed for President Roosevelt every single day. She took the time to pray for him again as she sat on the steps of her house. After all, on a day like today, he needed her prayers more than ever.

As she sat there, she bit her lip, deep in thought. Would the president decide that Americans should enter the war? Would American men have to fight? If so, would that mean Papa might have to leave? Tears rose to cover her eyelashes as she thought about it. What if Papa and the other men from Mexia had to leave—had to go to the other side of the world to fight in battles with the Japanese, Italians, and the Germans?

Something else occurred to her too.

"What if the war comes here…to Mexia?" she whispered. Would the fighting men from Europe come to their little farm and try to steal it away from them?

Worse yet, what if they flew their airplanes over and dropped bombs like they'd done at Pearl Harbor? What would she and her family and the others in her town do?

Eleanor Jo shivered as she thought about it all. How awful it would be to have something so terrible happen.

Several minutes later, Papa called out their names, and they ran quickly back to the house.

"Can you tell us now, Papa?" Martha Ann asked, breathlessly. "We want to know."

"Yes, darling, I'll tell you now."

With a sad look on his face, Papa told them the whole story. "There is a place in in Hawaii called Pearl Harbor," he explained, "where American military men live and work aboard battleships. Those good men were sleeping aboard their ships this very morning when the Japanese attacked unexpectedly, killing over two thousand of them And over a thousand more were wounded!"

As he spoke, Eleanor Jo remained silent but kept a watchful eye on her little brother and sister. Martha Ann looked a bit confused, as if she didn't quite understand what their father was saying. James listened to the story with wide eyes, as though Papa were telling them some sort of made-up tale from a storybook.

But it wasn't made up. Oh, how Eleanor Jo wished it were. How she wished she could ask the clock to go backward in time, to start the day all over again. Maybe then, things would go back to normal, back to the way they were before anyone ever mentioned that awful word—war.

"You see, Eleanor Jo, food is in short supply all across this country. People everywhere are rationing—cutting back, doing without—so that we can send food to our fighting men and to the poor people in Europe who are starving."

THE WAR EFFORT

SPRING, 1942

ORDINARILY, ELEANOR JO LOVED HER LIFE
on the dairy farm, especially when the cool
breezes of late winter turned warm and the
spring sunshine splashed across her face. That year, she
tried not to let her fears about the war dampen her love
of the new season.

The colorful azaleas Mama had planted along the
edge of the house had sprouted to life, and their lovely
pink color made Eleanor Jo's heart sing. Some days, to
make mealtimes special, she was allowed to pick a few
and bunch them together in a vase for the kitchen table.
Oh, how she enjoyed looking at those pretty pink petals.

She also loved to look at her mother's hand-stitched
quilts hanging out on the clothesline. The Dutch doll

was her personal favorite. She loved the friendship quilt too, with its colorful pattern. Then again, all of Mama's masterpieces were beautiful. And how fun it was when Mama's friends came over for a day of quilting!

"I love the springtime!" Eleanor Jo's little brother James shouted one day as he ran around the yard in his bibbed overalls after a light rain. Eleanor Jo knew it was true. Why, every weekend he ran around in his bare feet, throwing balls, chasing the dogs, and getting muddy from head to foot.

"You're getting mud all over my kitchen floor!" Mama would always tell him. Then she would wink at him as she cleaned him off. Afterward, she would mop the floor, all the while singing a lovely hymn.

James wasn't the only one who liked to act rowdy in the springtime. Eleanor Jo loved to watch the farm animals romp and play in the fields, particularly the noisy baby goats and the young calves, wobbling on their unsteady legs. She could watch them for hours on end. She also loved looking on as Papa milked the cows and fed the chickens and hogs before heading out to the oil fields to work. He knew just what it took to make a farm run smoothly, and she enjoyed looking on as he worked. What a hard worker her papa was!

Springtime brought something else new to the farm that year. A new batch of black and white puppies arrived in early April, just after Easter.

"Eleanor Jo, come look!" Martha Ann said with glee. She took Eleanor Jo by the hand and ran with her to the back of the barn. "I've named each one!"

"Oh?" Eleanor Jo couldn't help but giggle at her sister's enthusiasm.

"Yes." Martha Ann pointed. "This one is Shadrach. That one is Meschach, and the little one is Abednego."

"What about the girl puppies?" Eleanor Jo asked.

"I think I'll name them…" Martha Ann thought for a moment. "I'll call them Rachel and Leah."

Eleanor Jo laughed at her sister's great joy over the new bundle of puppies. Martha Ann enjoyed carrying them around in her little woven basket and singing silly songs to them as she did her chores. Eleanor Jo couldn't help but giggle. She loved the puppies too, cuddling them against her neck and giving them tiny kisses on their soft heads.

James seemed confused by the puppies' arrival. "But our dogs, Luke and Maggie, aren't married," he argued. "How can they have puppies?"

"Dogs don't get married," Mama tried to explain.

But, James insisted they should.

"We're going to have a dog wedding—right away!" he said. "We'll invite all of the children in the neighborhood."

Eleanor Jo and Martha Ann played along just for fun. Eleanor Jo invited their friends, and before long, the barn was full of neighborhood children, ready to watch the dogs get married.

"Luke looks handsome in your shirt, James," one of the little girls said with a giggle.

"Thank you," he said, taking a low bow.

"And Maggie looks pretty in my blouse, don't you think?" Martha Ann said with a sigh. "What a beautiful bride she is!"

"I've borrowed Mama's coffee table flowers for the wedding bouquet," Martha Ann said, presenting them.

"And I'll play the role of the minister!" James said with a serious look on his face. He put Papa's Sunday hat on his head, carried in a big Bible, and began to sing "Here Comes the Bride." Then, in his best minister voice, he carried on with the ceremony. Afterward, he pretended to put a ring on Maggie's finger.

"It won't fit!" he said with a sigh.

Eleanor Jo would never forget how they all giggled after James said, "I now pronounce you dog husband and dog wife!" Having fun like this always made her feel better about everything that was going on, on the other side of the world.

The war. Oh, how she hated to think about it.

In spite of every good thing—her schoolwork, her friends, her church, the farm, the puppies—one terrible problem remained. Their country was at war. Though she tried, she could not stop thinking about it. She could close her eyes and pretend it wasn't happening, but that wouldn't change a thing.

Late one night when she was nearly asleep, a plane flew over the house, and she trembled all over. "Lord, please protect us!" she prayed. "Don't let us be bombed!"

She called out for Mama. When her mother entered the room, she drew close and comforted Eleanor Jo. "It's just the mail plane, headed to Dallas," she assured her.

Still, it made Eleanor Jo nervous every time she heard a plane. So she continued to pray that the Lord would protect them all.

Nearly every evening, just before bed, Mama and Papa sat in front of the big radio, listening to the news reports. They also read about the war in the newspaper. Some of the headlines were very frightening, like the one that said "Mexia Citizens Receive Heroic Send-off."

The article went on to talk about several men and boys from her town who had gone off to fight. She knew all of them—her best friend Patricia's big brothers, Billy and Eugene, for instance, and Mr. Townsend, the man who ran the grocery store. They and many others had gone off to fight in the Pacific. Would they ever return home again?

Eleanor Jo sighed as she thought about Mary Lou, one of the older girls from church. Her boyfriend Bob was being shipped out next week, so they had decided to get married quickly before he left. Pastor Lewis was happy to perform the ceremony, but, how awful, to have your husband leave for war less than a week after your wedding! Yet it seemed to be happening all over the country.

There were other men shipping off too—men she knew quite well. Eleanor Jo sighed as she thought about Uncle Welton, Mama's younger brother. He was drafted right after the war started. Drafted, Papa had explained, was when you are told you *must* join the armed forces, whether you want to or not. Uncle Welton had chosen to be in the Air Force and was stationed at Love Field in Dallas. Thank goodness, he hadn't had to go to Europe or the Pacific to fight. But David Martin, her cousin, had been stationed in Europe on the battlefront. Oh, how she prayed he would be all right. He was such a handsome man.

Eleanor Jo shuddered, just thinking about the brave fighting men. Every night before going to bed, she prayed for their safety, and every night she had one special request: *Please, Lord, don't let my daddy leave.* Many times, Mama had assured her, that wouldn't happen. She explained that most of the men fighting in the war were younger than Papa. Still, Eleanor Jo couldn't help but worry and wonder. What would her family do if he had to go? Could Mama manage the farm without him? And what if something terrible happened to him, something like what had happened to those brave men in

Pearl Harbor? She couldn't even imagine life without her papa.

Eleanor Jo worked up the courage to ask Papa about these things one spring afternoon when he arrived home from the oil fields. Though she tried not to cry, the tears seemed to tumble down her cheeks as she posed the question, "Papa, will you have to leave us? Will you have to fight?"

He gathered her into his arms for a warm hug and then wiped away her tears. "I won't be going off to war, darling," he assured her. "So rest your pretty little head. I'll stay right here on the farm. There's plenty of work here to keep me busy, for sure." He looked her in the eye with a serious expression on his face. "But just because we're here, far away from where the fighting is taking place, doesn't mean we shouldn't do our part. We can all join in the war effort."

"War effort?" She gazed up into his eyes as she asked the question. "What do you mean?"

"Well…," he replied, giving her a knowing look, "we can pray for our soldiers, of course. But there are several practical things we can do, as well. I'm doing my best to cut back on gasoline by driving less, and we can conserve everyday things like tinfoil."

"Really? Will that really make a difference?" Eleanor Jo couldn't believe it.

"Oh yes," he explained. "Many of our local men are going down to Houston to work in factories where warships will be built."

Her eyes grew large. "Building warships? Like the ones in Pearl Harbor?" When Papa nodded, she asked, "But what does tinfoil have to do with building ships?"

"Every bit of scrap metal will help," he explained. "We will save even the smallest pieces. Of course, the government will also need rubber for making tires, so we want to make sure our shoes last as long as possible. We might have to resole them ourselves."

"Yes, Mama told me that."

A worried look came into his eyes as he told her the next thing. "Of course, there is the shortage of milk to be considered."

"There is a milk shortage, Papa?" Eleanor Jo asked.

"Yes," he explained. "Instead of raising cows, dairy farmers all across this country are using their land to grow crops. That means our little dairy farm is more important than ever. If we don't keep a steady supply of milk, people in town might resort to drinking powdered milk instead. And we don't want that to happen."

Eleanor Jo made a face. Yes, when you mixed up the white powder with water, it *looked* like milk, but it certainly didn't *taste* like the wonderful milk their cows produced.

She thought about that a moment. Perhaps she should offer to help Papa tend to the milking, or maybe there were other ways she could help out with the war effort.

"What can I do, Papa? I want to do something," she said earnestly.

He thought about it for a moment before answering. "You can help your mama plant a Victory garden," he said finally.

"A Victory garden? What is that?"

He smiled. "That's just a fancy name for a vegetable garden. Some people call it a war garden. We will grow the usual things: string beans, radishes, peppers, tomatoes, and so forth." His face took on a serious look. "You see, Eleanor Jo, food is in short supply all across this country. People everywhere are rationing—cutting back, doing without—so that we can send food to our fighting men and to the poor people in Europe who are starving."

Tears came to Eleanor Jo's eyes as she thought about it. She had watched Mama use their ration stamps to buy limited supplies of canned goods and meats at the grocery store. She didn't mind doing without some of her favorite things—like sugar, for instance—so that the fighting men could have enough to eat. Mama didn't seem to mind, either. Of course, James grumbled a bit, but that was to be expected. He was just a little boy, after all.

Papa grinned. "As long as we are willing to work hard to keep a garden, and to raise chickens and hogs, we won't go without food, that's for sure. The Bible says in 2 Chronicles 15:7, *Be ye strong therefore, and let not your hands be weak: for your work shall be rewarded.* And we will make sure others don't do without, either."

Eleanor Jo knew her father was a generous man. He often gave away milk to their neighbors who couldn't afford to pay for it. He also gave pigs and cows to the pastor. He believed in giving of his time, talents, *and* treasures. She wanted to be just like him when she grew up. She wanted to be known as a hard worker and a generous person who always put others first.

Right then and there, she decided she would do her part for the war effort. "I will help Mama with the Victory garden," Eleanor Jo said seriously. "But what else can I do?"

Papa rubbed his chin as he thought about it. "I know!" he said at last. "Perhaps you and your friends could write letters to the soldiers to let them know you are praying for them. It would help boost their morale and remind them that folks back home care about their well-being. How would that be?"

"Oh, what a wonderful idea! I will gather all of my friends together, and we will do that very thing!" She turned back toward the house, excited about the possibility. But before she reached the house, Papa called her name. "Yes, Papa?"

He gave her a warm smile as he said, "I'm so proud of you, Eleanor Jo."

She ran back to him and threw her arms around him. "Oh, Papa, I'm proud of you too. You and Mama both work *so* hard, and helping out is the least I can do. Thank you for telling me how I can help. I can hardly wait to begin!"

As she headed back to the house to gather her friends together to write letters, she suddenly felt as if she could make a difference in the war effort, a *real* difference. She could hardly wait to start. And she knew she wanted to do more too…she just didn't know what yet.

Keep the Home Fires Burning,
* while your hearts are yearning,*
Though your lads are far
* away they dream of home.*
There's a silver lining through
* the dark clouds shining,*
Turn the dark cloud inside out
* 'til the boys come home.*

KEEP THE HOME FIRES BURNING

JUNE, 1942

ELEANOR JO'S PARENTS WORKED HARDER than ever that summer to keep the dairy farm running smoothly and to lift the spirits of all who came and went from their home. Because Papa liked to start the day out right with a Bible verse and a prayer, each morning at the breakfast table he would quote 2 Chronicles 15:7, "*Be ye strong therefore, and let not your hands be weak: for your work shall be rewarded.*" Soon, the verse became their family motto.

Mama always loved to sing. One morning as she worked, she sang a song called "Keep the Home Fires Burning." Eleanor Jo listened carefully to the words as her mother's beautiful voice rang out.

"They were summoned from the hillside, they were
    called in from the glen,
And the country found them ready at the stirring call
    for men.
Let no tears add to their hardships as the soldiers pass
    along,
And although your heart is breaking make it sing this
    cheery song:

"Keep the Home Fires Burning, while your hearts are
    yearning,
Though your lads are far away, they dream of home.
There's a silver lining, through the dark clouds shining,
Turn the dark cloud inside out 'til the boys come home.

"Overseas there came a pleading, 'Help a nation in
    distress.'
And we gave our glorious laddies, honour bade us do
    no less,
For no gallant son of freedom to a tyrant's yoke should
    bend,
And a noble heart must answer to the sacred call of
    'Friend.'

"Keep the Home Fires Burning, while your hearts are
    yearning,
Though your lads are far away they dream of home.
There's a silver lining through the dark clouds shining,
Turn the dark cloud inside out 'til the boys come home."

When her mother finished the song, she had tears in her eyes, and Eleanor Jo couldn't help but ask, "What does it mean, Mama? What is the song about?"

Her mother smiled as she answered. "To keep the home fires burning means that we keep working here in America until our men return home again. We don't let our lamps go out."

"Lamps?"

"Yes, honey. Remember what the Bible says—that we should let our lights shine brightly?"

"Yes ma'am."

"One of the ways we do that is by working hard, just like the Bible says. *Be ye strong therefore, and let not your hands be weak: for your work shall be rewarded.* We do our part."

Mama's eyes grew misty as she said, "It also means that we never forget our fighting men and the sacrifice they are making for others. We pray for them, and we long for them to return to us, safe and sound. I'm so proud of you and your friends for writing letters to the soldiers. I know that means a lot to them."

Eleanor Jo pushed back the lump in her throat and tried not to cry...and she determined in her heart to do just what Mama was talking about. She *would* keep the home fires burning, and she would work extra hard, just like her parents.

So Eleanor Jo began looking for more opportunities to help out. She started by helping Papa around the farm. Besides collecting eggs each morning like she always did, she worked alongside Mama in the Victory garden each day, even on the hot days when the summer sun blazed down. She didn't mind getting hot and dirty, not when she thought about the men overseas who were working so hard to protect her freedom.

Why, there were plenty of things she could do! A couple of times, just for fun, Eleanor Jo helped Papa milk the cows. At least, she *tried* to help.

"Is this how you do it?" she asked her papa, trying to do it exactly as he had done.

The cow, a pretty brown and white named Mellie, didn't want to cooperate. She kicked over the bucket before even a drop could go into it!

"Oops! Sorry!" Eleanor Jo said with a sigh.

Papa laughed and ended up doing much of the work on his own, but he didn't seem to mind.

"I'll just watch," Eleanor Jo said with a shrug.

Afterward, Papa put the milk in large cans, which he then placed in water troughs in the watershed. That's where the water pump to the well was located.

"The cans will stay cool here," Papa explained, "until it's time to set them on State Highway 14 for the milk hauler to pick up."

After figuring up how much he was owed for the milk, Papa received a check. Eleanor Jo dreamed of one day running a dairy farm like her father. Oh, if only she could figure out how to milk those cows!

Some days, when her work was done and things were quiet and still, she would walk for miles in the pasture, beyond the narrow trickling stream to the far side of their property. She would go by herself, enjoying the beauty of God's green earth, thinking about the war on the other side of the world. How could things be so peaceful here, when they were so terrible over there? As she walked, she would pray for all of those brave men who were fighting to protect her freedom, and she would think about that song Mama sang, especially the part that said,

Keep the Home Fires Burning, while your hearts are
*   yearning,*
Though your lads are far away, they dream of home.
There's a silver lining, through the dark clouds shining,
Turn the dark cloud inside out 'til the boys come home.

She always found her eyes were full of tears after thinking about the words, especially when she thought about her cousin, David.

"Lord, please keep him safe!" she would pray.

She tried to look for the silver lining, just like the song said, but it was hard. One day this war would be over, and life would return to normal. Oh, she could hardly wait!

Sometimes Eleanor Jo would walk quite a distance beyond the stream, and she would end up on the back-side of the farm where Aunt Ella lived. Of course, Aunt Ella wasn't *really* her aunt. She was an elderly woman with the richest black skin Eleanor Jo had ever seen and eyes the color of James's darkest marbles. Aunt Ella worked with Papa on the farm. She also made corn shuck chair bottoms, and Eleanor Jo loved to watch her work.

Seemed like everyone on the farm stayed busy that summer. Mama worked especially hard in the garden, and Eleanor Jo and Martha Ann helped out as much as possible. After the vegetables were harvested, Mama and the children sat around in the cool of the morning and shelled peas, shucked and cut corn, and peeled ripe, golden peaches.

"This is my favorite part of the day," Mama would say. "Before it gets too hot out."

"It's my favorite too," Eleanor Jo would add.

Her brother and sister would just giggle. When Martha Ann or little James got caught throwing peas or slacking off, they were scolded immediately. Wasting food was never allowed. Not with so many doing without.

One day after lunch, Mama surprised the children by telling them they could play for a couple of hours before afternoon chores began. Excited, the three children ran off toward the field until they found their favorite spot. They giggled as they plopped down on the soft, green grass. The summer sun warmed their cheeks.

Eleanor Jo leaned back against the grass and stared at the beautiful blue sky above. The clouds were as white as cotton balls and seemed to float by as if they hadn't a care in the world.

"Tell me again—what are we doing?" Martha Ann asked, interrupting the quietness of the moment.

"We're watching the clouds. If you look close enough, you can see pictures in them."

"But I don't see anything!" Martha Ann argued.

"Look harder." Eleanor Jo stared up at the fluffy white clouds, almost sure she could see a pretty little lamb drift by. "Concentrate."

"*Concentrate*?" Little James echoed. "What's *concentrate*?" He rolled over in the grass, his striped overalls smudged with dirt, his bare feet waving in the wind.

"It means to pay attention," Eleanor Jo scolded. She tucked a strand of loose honey-brown hair behind her ear as she continued. "You know what it means to pay attention, don't you?"

"Yes," her brother and sister both said with a sigh.

They rested their heads back against the grass again and stared in silence at the sky. After a few moments of saying nothing, Martha Ann asked a question. "Do you think God is up there in heaven?"

"He is," Eleanor Jo said with a nod.

"So, Jesus is in heaven too?" Martha Ann asked. "He lives up there…way above the clouds?"

"Yes, He lives in heaven," Eleanor Jo explained. "*And* He lives in our hearts."

"But how?" Martha Ann insisted. "How can He be in two places at once?"

"It's a *mystery*," Eleanor Jo whispered. "That's what Pastor Lewis says."

"A mystery," James echoed.

"I don't get it," Martha Ann said with a sigh.

"God is everywhere," Eleanor Jo explained. "And He created everything—the sky, the birds, the grass, even us!"

"Wow," James whispered. "He must be really big!"

Yes. God *was* really big. Eleanor Jo knew it was true. He was big enough to create the whole universe and big enough to answer every prayer she prayed, even the really huge ones. And there were some mighty big prayers going up these days. She thought about the war, and tears came to her eyes.

Right away, she dried her eyes as she remembered—God was surely listening to their prayers. Why, He made even the hard times fun. Maybe that's where

Mama had learned to have fun too—during the hard times.

Up in the sky, a cloud drifted by. It looked like a Christmas tree. For just a moment, Eleanor Jo was reminded of a wonderful childhood Christmas when someone in the community had filled the area under their tree with gifts. Oh, how the Lord had provided for their family in such a special, miraculous way. Yes, what a big God He was!

She smiled as she thought about how she had prayed a prayer that Christmas to ask Jesus to come and live in her heart. What a wonderful Christmas present that had been!

As she leaned back against the grass with the warm afternoon sun blazing overhead, Eleanor Jo's eyes grew heavy. She almost dozed off. Only the sound of her mother's voice ringing out across the yard roused her from her near slumber.

"Children! Where are you? Playtime is over. There are more chores to be done."

Martha Ann groaned and rolled over, facedown in the grass. "But I didn't see any pictures yet!"

"Did you use your imagination?" Eleanor Jo asked.

"Imagination?" Martha Ann sat up and shrugged. "I didn't know I had one!"

Eleanor Jo couldn't help but laugh as she stood to her feet and brushed the dirt from her dress. "Trust me, everyone in our family has an imagination, especially Mama! And now that there's a war on, we need to use our imaginations more than ever!"

She and the others began to run in the direction of the house, laughing all the way. When they arrived at the door, Mama met them with a smile. "There are chores to be done and laundry to be put away. Let's get busy, children!"

Mama clapped her hands, and her face lit up as she broke into the pretty grin Eleanor Jo loved. Yes, Mama sure knew how to make work fun. Even though she worked hard, she always made a game of things. No, there was nothing depressing about work in her family! Oh, if only everyone across the country could have Mama's good attitude—maybe spirits would be lifted! Mama sang a little song as they worked, and pretty soon the children joined in. Before long, the whole house was filled with music. Eleanor Jo liked this part best of all.

"Many hands make the load light," Mama said. She quoted the family scripture: "*Be ye strong therefore, and let not your hands be weak: for your work shall be rewarded.*" While she was saying it, everyone joined in. Even James knew the verse now and quoted it enthusiastically. Then Mama explained that Christians should always stay busy, working hard to accomplish their daily tasks with smiles on their faces. "Your work will be rewarded!" she said.

"Now, that's something to smile about!" All the children giggled as they did their chores.

Yes, Eleanor Jo's mother believed in hard work, to be sure! Why, she would never go to bed at night until the house was straight and clean, and all of the housework completed. And she never raised her voice either, even when she scolded. Eleanor Jo hoped to be just like her mama when she grew up, especially when it came to working hard and being kind to others.

Mama taught the children that work came before play. She also encouraged them to finish what they started. Then, when the chores were done, they could play to their hearts' content. Eleanor Jo didn't mind, because Mama always made work fun. She taught the children to play as they worked.

"It is only a matter of choice," Mama said. "You can choose to have fun, or I will make you work."

The laundry was Eleanor Jo's favorite chore. Mama called it playing post office. After washing their clothes and bedding in their gasoline-run washing machine, Mama and the girls would hang the laundry out to dry on a line in the back yard. Eleanor Jo loved the sight of fresh, clean sheets and towels blowing in the afternoon breeze. When everything was dry, they would bring it all in and fold it. Then Mama would place the laundry into her children's outstretched arms.

"Take these towels to Box 22!" Mama would say, winking as she handed the bundle to James. "Take these sheets to Box 23!" she would say to Eleanor Jo.

The children would scurry around the house, putting up the clean sheets and towels, all the while pretending they were delivering mail.

That day, Eleanor Jo hurried with her bundles, hoping she would deliver the most mail and win the game. What fun they had!

Of course, there was still plenty of time that summer for playing real games too. Eleanor Joe loved playtime after chores were done. She loved jumping rope and playing jacks. She and Martha Ann and James would also swing on the tire swing, which Papa had hung from the large oak tree in the yard. They could spend hours, just swinging away and day-dreaming.

Still, even as she relaxed and played, she couldn't stop thinking about the war on the other side of the world. What were the soldiers doing right now? Were the men from Mexia safe? And what about the others? Surely they were all working even harder than she was.

Knowing how hard they were working made her want to work harder still. She often thought about their family scripture, *Be ye strong therefore, and let not your hands be weak: for your work shall be rewarded.*

She would not give up, no matter what. Her hands would *not* be weak, and she would be rewarded! She would keep the home fires burning!

———⟫●⟪———

"Says here women are also working as journalists and photographers. Why, who knows? Before long, Eleanor Jo might be a news reporter, writing stories for the Mexia paper about the war!"

———⟫●⟪———

WOMEN AT WORK

ARLY ONE MORNING IN JULY THAT SUMMER, Eleanor Jo noticed Papa lingered longer than usual at the kitchen table, reading the morning paper. He seemed to be very interested in the story on the front page.

"Listen here," he said to Mama. "Looks like we're not the only ones working hard this summer."

"What do you mean?" Mama asked. She put down her dishtowel and joined him at the table to look at the newspaper. "What is happening?"

He pointed to a headline that read, "Women Join the War Effort." All of the family members drew near so that he could explain what it meant.

"It says here that women are joining the workforce by the thousands," he explained. "They are working in shipyards, lumber mills, steel mills, and so forth. They are taking on positions as mechanics and electricians in place of the men who have left to fight in the war."

"I can't imagine women working in jobs such as that," Mama said with a worried look on her face. "Do you mean to say that women are really working in factories and building war ships? Doing men's work?"

"Yes, that's what it says." He tapped on the paper. "The article says that women will be taking over most of the jobs usually held by men," Papa explained. "They will operate buses, tractors, street cars, and taxi cabs. Many will also take over running farms while their husbands, sons, and fathers are away."

A shiver ran down Eleanor Jo's spine as she thought about that. She didn't want Mama to have to take over the farm, and had continued to pray that her father would never be drafted like Uncle Welton or cousin David. How would her family manage the cows, mules, and other animals without Papa? Who would do the milking? And who would plow the fields?

Mama threw in her two cents worth. "I've heard about women volunteering to serve in the Red Cross and raise money for the war effort, but I never thought I'd see the day when women were working in mills and driving taxi cabs and buses."

"With so many men leaving, they have no choice. Someone has to run things, after all," Papa said with a grin.

"I suppose you're right," Mama said with a sigh. "But if the women go to work in factories and so forth, they will be mighty tired by the time they arrive home to tend to their children and their houses."

"No doubt," Papa said. "But tough times call for tough people."

"That's for sure," Mama echoed.

Papa looked back at the newspaper. "Says here women are also working as journalists and photographers. Why, who knows? Before long, Eleanor Jo might be a news reporter, writing stories for the Mexia paper about the war!"

Eleanor Jo thought about that for a moment, then grabbed a pencil and tablet right away. She went into her room, shut the door, and wrote a long article about how everyone could help out with the war effort. Afterward, she showed it to Mama, who proclaimed it was every bit as good as any article she'd ever seen in the newspaper. Eleanor Jo beamed with pride. She decided right then and there she would keep doing everything she could to help out. And she would continue to write too.

Many times over the summer, she thought about Papa's words: *Tough times call for tough people.* That phrase ran over and over again in Eleanor Jo's mind. If women all over the country were rolling up their sleeves and going to work, then she would too. But what could she do? What sort of jobs could she perform before school began that would really make a difference? She was already helping out extra at home and writing letters to some soldiers, but she wanted to do more.

After gathering together a group of her friends, an idea was born.

"We will form a Victory Club!" Eleanor Jo announced. "A service organization for kids like us who want to help out with the war effort."

"What a wonderful idea," her friends agreed.

Eleanor Jo was elected president of the club, and right away, she put everyone to work. "I will write a newsletter once a week to keep us all informed," she explained.

The children grew more excited by the minute.

"And we'll hold a scrap drive too," she announced.

"How will it work?" Eleanor Jo's friend Clydene asked.

"On the first Saturday in August, we will make the rounds from house to house with our wagons," Eleanor Jo explained.

"What will we put in them?" her friend Patricia asked.

"Scrap metal," Eleanor Jo said, remembering what her papa had told her. "Anything that can be used to make tanks, ships, and so forth. We will collect irons, rakes, bird cages, tinfoil—anything that's metal. And we will encourage the people to donate bigger items as well, things like bed rails, old push lawnmowers…those kinds of items."

"We can't carry *those* in our wagons!" Clydene said, her eyes growing wide.

"No, but Papa says there are organizations that will come and carry off such things," Eleanor Jo explained. "People just have to pull their bigger items out to the ends of their driveways and civil defense workers will come by and pick them up. The main idea is to get people to think about donating the things they don't need, things that are just taking up space in their barns, closets, houses, and yards."

"What if people don't want to donate?" one of the girls asked.

"Then we'll say, 'Don't you know there's a war going on?'—just like the man on the radio says!" Eleanor Jo explained.

"Don't you know there's a war on?" they all cried in unison.

"This is brilliant, Eleanor Jo!" her friend Helen Bain said with a smile. "Why, with all of the families in Mexia pitching in, we will collect enough scrap metal to build a ship, I guarantee you! And maybe it will be the very ship that wins the war!"

All of the girls ooh'd and aah'd over that idea. How interesting to think that their old metal scraps could actually be melted down and made into something useful! Something to help in the war.

On the first Saturday in August, the big day for the scrap drive arrived. Many of the children in Mexia worked together, going door to door, pulling red wagons of every shape and size behind them. The summer heat made it difficult, but people along the way offered them cups of lemonade and water to quench their thirst.

At every stop she made, Eleanor Jo greeted the people with the words "V for Victory!" and made the victory sign with her hand—separating her index finger and middle finger into a "V." Folks would return the sign and respond with the same words, "V for Victory!" The children raced up and down the streets, pulling their red wagons and shouting the Victory cheer.

By the end of the day, all of the children and their parents met up at the church with wagons and wagons overflowing with scrap metal, which the civil defense workers picked up.

"I'm so proud of you, Eleanor Jo, I could bust a button!" Mama said with a smile.

Eleanor Jo was tickled to think she'd made her mother proud, but more than that…she felt good about the fact that she had been able to help out in some way.

She wrote all of the stories down for the weekly newsletter, detailing everything the children had done. Soon everyone in the whole town of Mexia knew about the Victory Club and was singing their praises.

But the work didn't stop there. Though the summer was almost over, there was one more thing Eleanor Jo wanted the Victory Club members to do before school started. She got the idea from her mother.

"We will hold a fundraiser for the American Red Cross and give a prize to the girl who collects the most money!" she explained. They would go around to all of the businesses in Mexia, asking them to donate money to the American Red Cross.

"Wonderful!" Helen said.

"Marvelous!" Clydene agreed.

Mr. Jenkins, who ran the five and dime, offered the prize—a beautiful red and black autograph book. All of the girls wanted to win it, and Eleanor Jo was curious to see who would work the hardest to receive it.

The second Saturday in August, the girls and their mothers went from business to business, both in Mexia and in the nearby town of Teague, asking for donations. They visited every shop, every store, every gas station, and every place of business—all in an attempt to collect money for the American Red Cross.

"Give to the Red Cross!" the children's voices rang out. "Give to soldiers in need!"

"I'll give," said the man in the butcher shop.

"I'll give too," said the woman cutting fabric at the five and dime. "My nephew is fighting, so I will be happy to donate!"

"I'll come by the church and donate blood later in the month," several others said.

Donating blood was important during wartime, for many of the wounded soldiers would not live otherwise.

So many times along the way, Eleanor Jo and her mother met up with someone who had a son, brother, or father serving in the armed forces. Each time, they paused to pray. Mama's voice trembled as she offered up prayers right and left. And the words "V for Victory!" rang out again and again as they moved on to the next place.

At the end of the day, when all the money had been counted, they discovered that Clydene had won the contest. Eleanor hugged her friend. She was so happy she had won. Clydene was the best friend in all the world.

Clydene whooped and hollered. "I won! I won!" She held the little autograph book up in the air and announced, "This is the best prize I've ever received in my twelve years of living!"

All the girls gathered round to get a closer look. Right away, Clydene asked all of the girls to sign it. Eleanor Jo wrote the words *V for Victory!* and then signed her name, along with the date: *Eleanor Jo Bozeman, August 14, 1942.*

"I am so happy for you, Clydene!" Eleanor Jo exclaimed. "This has been one of the best days of the summer."

The autograph book was a nice prize, of course, but Eleanor Jo decided the best gift really had nothing to do with prizes. The best gift of all was being able to give back—of her time and her energies—like other women across America were doing. To help others in need. That was the best gift any girl could give, especially during times such as these.

"Your hair looks just lovely, Eleanor Jo. And my, how grown up you look."

A New Year,
a New Look

FALL OF 1942

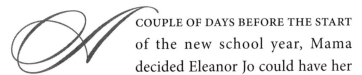

COUPLE OF DAYS BEFORE THE START of the new school year, Mama decided Eleanor Jo could have her hair curly like she had always wanted. She took Eleanor Jo to the beauty parlor to have a permanent put into her hair. Eleanor Jo could hardly believe it! She wasn't sure if she should be excited or nervous. After all, she'd never had a permanent before.

Once they arrived, she sat up straight in the chair and watched as the hairdresser, Mr. Kurly Hopson, a tall man with a wrinkled brow, thinned her hair and then applied a very gooey, smelly solution to it. Her eyes began to sting, and her scalp burned. Hopefully, this part wouldn't last long. The fellow reached for a basket of metal hair rollers and started rolling her wet hair, one section at a time.

"Ouch!" She tried not to complain, but all of the pulling and tugging hurt her scalp. Did she have to go through all of this, just to have pretty curls like Mama and her sister?

Eleanor Jo breathed a sigh of relief when the hair-dresser finally finished the rolling process. He gestured for her to stand and then led her to a row of chairs along the wall.

"Oh, my goodness, do I have to?" She stared in amaze-ment at a tall machine with electric wires hanging from it. It looked a little scary, to be honest, and she wasn't sure she wanted to be plugged in, even if it made her the prettiest girl in all of Mexia.

The hairdresser hooked up the electric wires to her curlers, and she held her breath, to see if she would be electrocuted. No, everything was just fine. Still, she felt a bit like a creature from one of her little brother's comic books, but she didn't say so. How could she, when Mama sat nearby, smiling like that? No, she would go along with it, and hope in the end she turned out looking like one of those movie stars whose pictures hung in front of the movie theater down the street.

Less than an hour later, Eleanor Jo stared into the mirror in disbelief. Was the reflection staring back at her really hers? Could it be? "Oh, Mama!" she whispered.

"What do you think?" the hairdresser asked.

She reached up with her hand and patted her tight curls. "Well…," she stammered, "it's…it's so different!"

And it was! She wasn't sure if she could get used to the curls.

"For some reason, it still feels like there are rollers in my hair, tugging away."

"It will feel like that for a while," Mama explained.

Eleanor Jo groaned. Her whole head ached. And it still smelled funny from the solution too. Would it be like this forever?

"You look beautiful, Eleanor Jo," Mama said proudly.

That brought a smile to Eleanor Jo's face. If Mama thought she looked pretty, surely others would think the same. So perhaps it was worth a little pain to be beautiful.

They left the beauty salon and headed toward J.C. Penney, where Miss Chandler's mother worked. Miss Polly Chandler had been Eleanor Jo's second grade teacher.

Going to the department store with mother was always fun, but shopping during wartime was a little harder.

"You can only purchase one pair of shoes," Mama reminded her.

"I know." Eleanor Jo drew in a sigh and didn't say anything else. Once again, she didn't want to complain.

After all, Mama surely knew what it meant to sacrifice. She couldn't purchase any items without ration stamps.

"I promised to buy you one store-bought dress before school starts," her mother reminded her, "as well as underclothes and socks, and even additional fabrics so that more dresses can be made."

They walked through the large glass door, and Mrs. Chandler met them in the girls' department.

"Well, hello!" She smiled when she saw Eleanor Jo's hair and complimented her on it right away. "Your hair looks just lovely, Eleanor Jo. And my, how grown up you look." Then she led them to a rack of new dresses.

"Ooo! I like the yellow plaid," Eleanor Jo said, pointing. "It looks so bright and cheery. Like a beautiful summer day."

"That will look lovely with your new hairstyle," Mrs. Chandler agreed.

Mama went to the fabric section, looking over the colorful bolts.

"What colors do you like?" she asked.

"I like red!" Eleanor Jo said. "And pink, of course. And that green is pretty!" she pointed to a lovely bolt of colorful green fabric. "I guess I like them all."

Her mother selected several yards of bright-colored fabrics, along with other items. Soon they paid for their goods and thanked Mrs. Chandler for all of her help.

She gave Eleanor Jo a wink and once again told her how pretty she looked.

Eleanor Jo thought about that all the way home. With her new dress and hairdo, she looked more like Mama. Just the thought of it made her feel grown up.

She still felt that way a couple of days later as she dressed for her first day of school. "I can't believe I will be in the sixth grade this year," she said to herself.

She wore her new yellow dress, of course, and spent extra time getting her hair just right. The curls had relaxed a little and fell in soft waves around her face. She put in her favorite barrettes to keep the hair out of her eyes. She loved school and wanted everything to be perftect.

As she came in for breakfast, Papa complimented her and so did Martha Ann. Growing up was fun, especially when folks noticed you were changing.

Eleanor Jo was so excited about the new school year starting, she could hardly eat her breakfast. Minutes later, after saying goodbye to her parents, she, walked with Martha Ann and James to the bus stop. All three children carried black lunch boxes. In her pocket, Eleanor Jo placed the nickel that Mama had given her for ice cream.

Clydene met her at the bus stop at the edge of the farm. She took one look at Eleanor Jo's new curls and clapped her hands in glee. "You look bee-you-tee-ful!" she proclaimed.

Eleanor Jo giggled. "Why, thank you very much!"

Just then, a rooster let out a squawk. Clydene squealed and grabbed Eleanor Jo's arm.

"Remember how that mean old rooster chased me around last year?" Clydene said with wide eyes.

Eleanor Jo nodded, remembering. Many times last spring that mean old rooster had chased them around and flapped his wings, pecking at their feet. Clydene had actually prayed that Jesus would come back so that she wouldn't have to fight the crazy rooster again this year. But here he was, clawing at the ground and scratching up dust.

"Hurry, Eleanor Jo, hurry!" Clydene screamed, taking her by the arm.

Thankfully, the school bus arrived quickly, and they climbed aboard. As Eleanor Jo took her seat, she thought about the year ahead.

"Sixth grade is going to be hard," she said with a sigh.

"Not for you," Clydene said. "You're such a good student."

"We'll see." Hopefully, Eleanor Jo could keep her grades up and still help around the farm too. She also knew this school year would be different from others, because of the war. Surely the students would all join in the Victory Club, working together as a team to support their troops.

Once they arrived at the school, all of her friends gathered around to have a look at her new hairdo. They ooh'd and aah'd with curious smiles on their faces.

"Ooo, you look just like Lana Turner," Patricia said, as she reached to touch Eleanor's curls.

"No, she looks like Rita Hayworth!" Helen argued. "I saw her picture down at the Majestic Theater. "She's in a new movie called *Tales of Manhattan*, and her hair is beautiful, just like Eleanor Jo's!"

"No, she looks like Eleanor Powell," Clydene threw in. "I saw her in *Broadway Melody*. She's one of my favorite actresses, and Eleanor Jo even has her name!"

On and on the girls went, comparing her to popular movie stars. Eleanor Jo couldn't help but smile, though she had never seen a movie at the theater like most of the other girls. Did she really look like a Hollywood starlet?

"I think she looks dreamy," Clydene added, "and very grown up. I wish I had curls like that."

Just then, Mrs. Munger, the principal, passed by. She turned back and stared at her with a look of amazement in her eyes. "Why, I hardly recognized you, Eleanor Jo. You're looking quite grown up."

"Thank you," she said with a smile.

She linked one arm through Patricia's and the other through Clydene's, and with Helen tagging along behind, they made their way down the hallway toward the class-room. They entered the sixth grade room, where their teacher Mrs. Yelldell awaited them. Eleanor Jo already missed Mrs. Evans, her teacher from last year, but looked forward to a brand-new year with a new teacher. She also hoped she could keep up her perfect attendance record which she had managed to keep for four years in a row.

"Let's stand to say the Pledge of Allegiance!" the teacher instructed.

As Eleanor Jo put her hand to her heart, she thought about what it meant to be patriotic, to love her country. Naturally, that made her think about the war on the other side of the world. Just the thought of it brought tears to her eyes.

After the pledge, Mrs. Yelldell took attendance then smiled at her new students. "Welcome to a new year, everyone!" she exclaimed. Next, she walked to the black-board and wrote the date: *September 9, 1942.* As she turned back to the classroom, she said, "I will teach you a little trick so that you can always remember what year it is. Columbus discovered America in 1492, and this is 1942. If you can remember one, you will remember the other."

Eleanor Jo wrote the dates down in her tablet, knowing she would never forget them. To think! In 1492, Columbus was traveling in a ship, ready to discover this new land. And now, in 1942, brave men were traveling by ship to other parts of the world to fight for her freedom. How very interesting.

The more she thought about it, the more Eleanor Jo realized lots of things were new and different this year, not just her hair and her clothes.

Oh, if only she could change things on the other side of the world as easily as she had changed her hairdo and her wardrobe. Then, *everything* would be just perfect.

―――⇒●⇐―――

"Eleanor Jo, you need to learn that there is a lemon in every crowd. You are sweet enough; you must learn to make lemonade. Just add a spoonful of sugar, and every problem will turn into an opportunity."

―――⇒●⇐―――

MAKING LEMONADE

THANKSGIVING, 1942

A FEW WEEKS INTO THE NEW SCHOOL year, Mama took on a job working part-time as postmistress in Mexia. How perfect, since she loved playing post office with the laundry. Now she could really work in a post office!

Eleanor Jo was so excited about this news that she decided it was time she found a job too. But, where?

Mrs. Weaver, an older woman who ran the school cafeteria, needed someone to clean tables, empty trash cans, and mop the floors.

"This would be an excellent way to earn a little money!" Eleanor Jo said to her friend Patricia.

"You're right!" Patricia agreed. "And we will get to spend lots of time together too!"

Eleanor Jo took Patricia by the arm and whispered in her ear. "My papa says that women all over the country are going to work to help out during the war. We will work hard, like my Mama and so many other women are doing. We will make a difference for our families!"

"Yes!" Patricia's eyes grew large with excitement.

Eleanor Jo didn't mind the hard work, even though it meant cleaning up after messy students. She was full of energy and loved to stay busy. Besides, it was worth it all at the end of the week when she received thirty-five cents for her work. She also got free lunches, which was wonderful. Eleanor Jo didn't have to carry her lunchbox anymore. But best of all, she could now make donations to the Red Cross, herself.

One afternoon, she and Patricia were in the cafeteria cleaning tables. They thought they were doing a wonderful job until Mrs. Weaver came along with a sour look on her face. Exasperated, she threw a dishcloth at Eleanor Jo and proclaimed, "If I want it done right, I guess I'll just have to do it myself."

A lump grew up in Eleanor Jo's throat, and she knew she was going to cry. She didn't want to do so in front of Patricia, so she walked out into the hallway, where the tears flowed freely. She didn't know what she had done wrong, but she certainly knew Mrs. Weaver was disappointed in her, and that really hurt her feelings. The longer she thought about it, the more she cried.

Just then, the school principal, Mrs. Munger, came along. She was a tall, stately, and proper woman. She paused when she saw Eleanor Jo crying.

"Why, what has happened to bring such sadness?" Mrs. Munger asked with a concerned look on her face.

Eleanor wiped her eyes and told her the story with a sigh.

Afterward, Mrs. Munger said, "Eleanor Jo, you need to learn that there is a lemon in every crowd. You are sweet enough; you must learn to make lemonade. Just add a spoonful of sugar, and every problem will turn into an opportunity."

Eleanor Jo couldn't help but smile as she thought about that. Mrs. Weaver had been awfully sour, but that didn't mean *she* had to be. No, she could walk back into that cafeteria, put a smile on her face, and respond with kindness. That would add sweetness to the situation, after all.

And that's just what she did. Day after day, she worked alongside Patricia and Mrs. Weaver in the cafeteria, and after awhile, Mrs. Weaver grew nicer and nicer. Within weeks, she was one of Eleanor Jo's favorite people. Mrs. Munger had been right! You really *could* turn lemons into lemonade.

Eleanor Jo also remembered her family's favorite verse, *Be ye strong therefore, and let not your hands be weak: for your work shall be rewarded.* She wouldn't give up. Never! She would just go on, adding a spoonful of sugar everywhere she went.

Eleanor Jo had an opportunity to do just that the week before Thanksgiving.

After hearing about the Victory Club, Mrs. Yelldell decided all of the students in her history class could join in, writing letters of encouragement and thanks to the soldiers. There would also be a prize for the best letter written. Eleanor Jo had already written many letters to soldiers, but she was excited to write to someone new. She thrust her hand in the basket on Mrs. Yelldell's desk, wondering which name she would draw.

The man Eleanor Jo picked was named George Davis, a mechanic from the nearby town of Teague. She had never met Mr. Davis, but it turned out that Miss Chandler's mother knew him because his mother shopped at J.C. Penney. She told Eleanor Jo that George was a handsome young man, barely out of high school. He had been a star quarterback on the Teague High School team, but now he was fighting in the Pacific alongside thousands of other men.

All of the girls gathered together to talk about their soldiers. Eleanor Jo tried to picture what George Davis looked like.

"Maybe he's tall and strong with broad shoulders and an engaging smile," she told Clydene.

"And maybe he has wavy hair and dark eyes," Clydene replied.

"Or maybe he has blonde hair and blue eyes," Eleanor Jo thought out loud.

Regardless of his looks, he would surely love to have a letter from home—even though it would take several weeks to reach him. She would add a spoonful of sugar to his difficult situation.

So Eleanor Jo wrote the best letter she could. She thanked Mr. Davis for serving his country in the armed forces and told him that she would pray for him every night. She gave him the weather update in their area and told him the scores of the last few Teague High School football games, which she guessed he would really appreciate. Finally, she told him Mrs. Munger's story—about turning lemons into lemonade. If anyone needed to know how to do that, it was a soldier!

All of the students read their letters aloud during their history class.

"The prize goes to Eleanor Jo!" Mrs. Yelldell proclaimed. "It is the best in the group!"

Eleanor Jo could hardly believe it. "Th...thank you!" she stammered.

"As the winner, you will receive a picture of General Dwight Eisenhower, as well as an eagle flag of the United States," her teacher explained, placing the items in her arms.

Eleanor Jo could scarcely believe it! She was very proud of both—so much so, that she took them home to Papa.

"We will display them on the north wall of the living room," Papa proclaimed. And that is exactly what he did.

Every day Eleanor Jo looked at those things and was reminded that, with God's help, the whole country could take lemons and turn them into lemonade.

It wasn't always easy to be positive, especially when the war reports started coming in. It seemed so many people in town were affected by the war. Poor Mrs. Smith, the woman who worked in the library at the school—her son died in one of the battles. And Mr. Franklin, the man who used to run the bakery, was badly wounded and might never walk again. Right now, he was in a hospital on the other side of the world. But the good folks from Mexia sent him cards and letters by the dozen.

Perhaps one of the most amazing stories of all was the one about her cousin, David Martin. One night, Eleanor Jo's Aunt Vera awoke in the middle of the night with a burden to pray for David, which she did intently until the sun came up. Later, she learned that David had been involved in a battle and nearly died in a foxhole. Thank goodness, Aunt Vera listened to the voice of the Holy Spirit and prayed when she did! Eleanor Jo believed more now than ever that God answers prayers.

As Thanksgiving drew near, there were so many things for the people of Mexia to think and talk about. But Eleanor Jo didn't worry or fret. Every time she started to, she did her best to think happy thoughts, to focus on the good, and to do what Mrs. Munger had said.

On Thanksgiving Day as the family gathered around the table, everyone took turns telling what they were thankful for. When it was Eleanor Jo's turn, she smiled and said, "I'm thankful for lemons."

"Lemons?" everyone at the table spoke in unison. They looked around at each other curiously.

"Why lemons?" Mama asked.

"Because," Eleanor Jo said with a smile, "without lemons, there wouldn't be any lemonade."

Everyone stared at her with looks of confusion on their faces, but she just grinned. No, as long as she remembered that every problem was an opportunity to make something good out of bad, she would be just fine.

"Going to Mammy Powell's at Christmas is the best!" Eleanor Jo said with great excitement

---

A WARTIME
CHRISTMAS

HAT YEAR AT CHRISTMASTIME, Eleanor Jo looked forward to celebrating the holiday with her family and other relatives at her Mammy Powell's house. Mammy Powell was her mother's mother, and she lived in the town of Thornton, Texas. Sadly, Grandpa Powell had passed away years before, so Mammy Powell lived alone. But she loved it when people came for a visit, especially during the holidays when they could celebrate together. It seemed more important this year than ever, what with the war going on and all.

On the day before Christmas, the whole family climbed into the car to make the journey.

"Don't forget, Mammy Powell is nearly deaf," Eleanor Jo reminded Martha Ann as they drove along. "She has to wear hearing aids."

"How come?" Martha Ann asked with a wrinkle in her brow.

"She lost her hearing as a teen," Eleanor Jo explained, "when she had the measles."

"How sad!" Martha Ann said, leaning back against the car seat.

"Yes." Just the thought of it made Eleanor Jo sad. How awful it would be, not to be able to hear. Life would be very difficult indeed, especially when folks in the family got to telling stories, which they always did at Christmastime.

Still, it was fascinating to look at her grandmother's hearing aid. The battery was about the size of a deck of cards. Mammy Powell had sewn a little pocket for the battery and pinned it to her slip. How clever she was! Now, that was one woman who certainly knew how to turn lemons into lemonade!

In spite of her hearing loss, Mammy Powell was a hard worker, just like Mama and Papa. In fact, she was the one who had taught Mama to work hard. Mammy Powell's house was always as neat as a pin. Even her yard was swept clean. She did her laundry by hand in a large black wash pot and hung it out to dry on the clothesline in her backyard.

"I love going to Mammy Powell's house," Martha Ann said with a sigh.

"Me too," Eleanor Jo said. She had so many memories of the hours she had spent there, especially during the summertime. Mammy Powell would always give her money to purchase ice cream. Eleanor Jo would walk about ten blocks to Black's Drug store, where the clerk would pack a pint of her favorite flavor. Then she would walk back home, and they would have an ice cream party.

"Going to Mammy Powell's at Christmas is the best!" Eleanor Jo said with great excitement. At Christmas, the whole family came together to celebrate the birth of the Savior.

"And this is going to be the best Christmas ever because Uncle Welton is going to be with us!" Mama added.

When they arrived at Mammy Powell's, icicles covered the house. It was bitterly cold outside. Mammy Powell met them at the door with a smile. She was wearing a print apron over her starched green dress, and her white hair was pulled up on top of her head. Her royal blue tennis shoes caught Eleanor Jo's eye.

Mammy Powell waved and smiled, and Eleanor Jo could hardly wait to wrap her arms around her and give her a hug. Just then, Uncle Welton appeared in the doorway behind her. Eleanor Jo's heart swelled with joy as she saw him in his uniform. His short brown, wavy hair made him look a little different from usual, but he had the same sparkling blue eyes and playful smile as always. How handsome he looked! And how wonderful to have him here, safe and sound. Oh, if only all of the soldiers could come home for Christmas!

She ran in his direction and hugged him tightly.

"What? No hugs for me?" Mammy Powell said, with a pretend stern look on her face.

"Of course!" Eleanor Jo exclaimed, giving her grandmother a warm hug.

Everyone else in the family began to talk at once, welcoming Uncle Welton home. They made their way inside and pulled off their coats.

"Coffee for the grownups and hot chocolate for the children!" Mammy Powell announced.

All of the children gathered round and drank warm mugs of cocoa and nibbled at homemade teacakes, Eleanor Jo's favorite. Then they settled in the living room and asked Uncle Welton all sorts of questions.

"Tell us about life in Dallas!" Mama said.

"Yes, and tell us about the men serving overseas," Eleanor Jo added.

He shared what his life was like in Dallas, where he was stationed at Love Field. He spoke with great pride about the many men serving overseas, his eyes filling with tears each time he mentioned them. He also thanked the children for sending him postcards, and he pledged to keep every one.

Eleanor Jo couldn't help but notice the look of pride in Mammy Powell's eyes. It was obvious she loved her son so much. Mama seemed proud too. After all, Uncle

Welton was her younger brother and she loved him dearly.

The womenfolk went to the kitchen to tend to the food, and the men gathered around the fireplace to chat. Eleanor Jo took that opportunity to tell her uncle about the Victory Club, sharing all of the children's ideas.

"We're doing so many wonderful things, Uncle Welton," she said, proudly. "And we're having such a good time too."

He smiled broadly. "You're such a big help to our serving men, Eleanor Jo. I'm so proud of you. The troops are honored that the children of America are helping out so much. It's such a blessing."

"We want to do even more, Uncle Welton," Eleanor Jo said. "What do you suggest? Do you have ideas for things we can do, things that will really help?"

He paused to think for a moment, scratching his head. Suddenly his face lit up as an idea came to him. "What about savings bonds?" he suggested. "Even the president buys savings bonds!"

"Savings bonds?" She had never heard of such a thing, so she didn't know what to say.

"Yes, our country's leaders have arranged a way for people to help our fighting men by supplying money."

"Money?" Eleanor Jo wrinkled her nose. "I don't really have a lot of money."

"Yes, but you do earn a nickel here and there, don't you?" he asked.

"Yes, of course! I work in the school cafeteria. I make thirty-five cents a week," she said proudly. "I also earn little bit of money doing chores and helping others from time to time. I pay my tithes at church, and I donate some money to the Red Cross. I love to help out!"

"Great! Well, this is another way you can do that. Set aside an extra nickel or two a week until you have twenty-five cents saved up," he explained. "Then you can take that money to the post office where your mama works and get a little stamp, which you can paste in a book. It will take $18.75 worth of stamps to fill the book. When it's filled, you can trade it in for a savings bond."

"A savings bond." She pondered the words. "Then what?"

"That money—the $18.75—will be used to supply things for our troops such as uniforms, food, and so forth. You are helping a soldier when you buy a war bond."

"Wow!" Eleanor Jo thought about that for a moment. She would do it! And she would ask all of her friends to buy war bonds too! Why, what if every person in America bought just one? Think of how many soldiers could be helped!

She thought about this as everyone continued to visit. A little while later, the children asked, as they always did, if they could look in Mammy Powell's big quilt box in the living room. They always had such a good time picking through the colorful pieces of fabric and imagining beautiful quilts. This time, however, the children were surprised at what they found inside.

"What is this, Mammy Powell?" Martha Ann asked, holding up a gray scarf.

"Ah, that's part of my knitting campaign!" Mammy Powell said. "Have you not heard about that?"

All of the children shook their heads as their grandmother explained. "The American Red Cross has called on women across the country to knit scarves, hats, and so forth for our troops, to help keep them warm."

"What a wonderful idea!" Eleanor Jo said. Perhaps when she got home, she would tell all of the members of the Victory Club so that they could begin knitting too!

"We must choose blue or gray yarn," Mammy Powell went on, "to match the military uniforms. And we're not just knitting, either. Several of us are sewing bandages, and even pajamas."

"Really?"

"Yes, we're taking old sheets, boiling them in pots on the stove to make sure they're clean, and then cutting them down into smaller pieces just right for bandaging wounds.

Eleanor Jo thought about that for a minute. Several of her friends were wonderful seamstresses—Patricia and Helen, for example. And certainly members of the Victory Club had old sheets in their homes. Perhaps they could be persuaded to sew bandages for the soldiers too. What wonderful things the club members could accomplish if they would work together.

Just then, a joyous melody rang out, and the children looked across the room to discover Uncle Welton playing the piano. Eleanor Jo loved to hear the story of the wonderful old box grand piano which had once belonged to General Mexia. Eleanor Jo was to inherit the piano one day. She could hardly wait!

The family gathered around, and Uncle Welton led them in singing "Silent Night." His beautiful bass voice rang out, filling the tiny house. A shiver ran down Eleanor Jo's spine, though she didn't sing a single note.

Finally, her uncle turned to look at her. "Why aren't you singing, Eleanor Jo?" he asked.

She was too embarrassed to answer, so she simply shrugged.

He asked the question again. "C'mon, tell Uncle Welton. Why won't you sing?"

"My third grade music teacher told me I couldn't sing—that my voice wasn't very good."

"What?" He gave her a surprised look. "Why, I'm sure that's not true! Let's hear a note or two."

With his help, she sang the first line of the song, and right away, everyone began to applaud.

"Why, you have a lovely voice!" Uncle Welton said. "So don't get defeated when someone tells you something like that. Use their words to better yourself, but don't use them to get discouraged. Turn those sour old lemons into lemonade!"

Eleanor Jo couldn't help but giggle. Why, that was the very thing *she* always said now!

That night, the children went to bed early in anticipation of Christmas morning. Eleanor Jo could hardly sleep because she was so excited. In years past, especially during the difficult years of the Depression, there hadn't been many presents under the tree. This Christmas, presents would be limited as well, due to the war. But she didn't mind at all.

The following morning, the children awoke with squeals. They met in the living room, and Mama recited the Christmas story from the book of Luke. She told them about the shepherds and wise men, and then about the Christ-child, born in a manger. Afterward, with tears in her eyes, she said, "Children, we have so much to be thankful for. Jesus Christ came to the earth as a baby, but He grew into a man and took the sins of the world upon Himself on the cross at Calvary."

Eleanor Jo knew this story, of course, but loved to hear it again and again. As a youngster, she had prayed to ask Jesus to come and live in her heart. That made every

Christmas season even more special. She was a child of the King!

After Mama finished sharing the story, Papa prayed the most beautiful prayer Eleanor Jo had ever heard. Then the children began to open presents, their happy-go-lucky voices raised in glee. Eleanor Jo and Martha Ann were both delighted to see that they had received watches. James received a bicycle and a toy gun. Right away, he jumped up and pointed his gun at the others in the room, pretending he was in the war.

"You would be better served to play with that outside," Papa warned, knowing the sight of the gun upset Mammy Powell and Mama.

"Yes sir." He put it down with a sigh.

After opening the gifts, the children played outdoors while the womenfolk prepared their Christmas dinner. Eleanor Jo's mouth watered as she anticipated the foods: turkey, cornbread dressing, cranberry salad, yams, and string beans. And her favorite part of all—pumpkin pie. Yummy!

At noontime, the family gathered around the table which was now covered in casserole dishes and platters. The whole thing looked and smelled scrumptious! After Papa led them in prayer, the adults sat at the big table and the children sat nearby at a smaller one. The clacking of the knives and forks, along with the voices raised in joyous chatter, provided a musical sound that filled Eleanor Jo's ears. For a moment, she almost forgot there was a war going on on the other side of the world.

Then, she looked across the room and saw James's toy gun leaning against the edge of the sofa. Only then did she remember. And only then did she offer up yet another prayer for the safety of their fighting men.

"Yes, of course," Papa said. "That's what the Bible tells us to do. We are to pray for both our friends and our enemies."

POW CAMP

SPRINGTIME OF 1943

*T*HE NEXT FEW WEEKS, ELEANOR JO worked hard to earn extra nickels, which she saved in a handkerchief in her chest of drawers. Before long, she had five of them, and Papa took her to the post office where Mama worked so that Eleanor Jo could buy her first stamp for her savings bond book. She kept the book safe in her drawer and told all of her friends in the Victory Club about it so they could do the same.

She also told her friends about the sewing campaign, and many offered to cut up old sheets into bandages. Patricia was happy to head up that campaign since she was the best seamstress. And they all agreed to continue praying for the safety of the troops. What power their prayers must have had!

One morning, just as Eleanor Jo tucked the little savings bond book away in her drawer, she overheard Papa talking to Mama in the kitchen. He was telling her something about a camp that was being built nearby. Eleanor Jo could barely make out his words, but Mama's thoughts came through loud and clear. She didn't seem to like the idea…but why?

Eleanor Jo ran into the kitchen, excited. "A camp, Papa? Can we go?"

"No, Eleanor Jo." The look on his face let her know right away that this was not the kind of camp they would ever go to. "I'm talking about a prisoner of war camp that will soon open just a few miles away."

"Prisoner of war?" Eleanor Jo couldn't figure out what he meant.

"I don't understand," Mama said with a concerned look. "How is this possible? Why would they bring prisoners half-way across the world to Mexia? It doesn't make a bit of sense."

"I heard about it from several of the men in town," Papa said. "The Mexia Chamber of Commerce and city officials have given the go-ahead for a prisoner of war camp on government-owned property three miles west of town. It's already being built. The whole thing has been very hush-hush."

"That's mighty close to our house," Mama whispered, her eyes growing large.

"What is a prisoner of war camp?" Eleanor Jo asked, still unsure.

"Our soldiers have captured several German and Japanese prisoners," Papa did his best to explain. "And we cannot send those men back to their homes until after the war is over. So we must find a safe place for them to live and work until the war ends."

"But why here?" Eleanor Jo asked. "Why Mexia?" Nothing about this made sense to her.

"It has something to do with our climate being the best for the prisoners. That's why the government has chosen our area."

"I don't want the prisoners here, Papa," Eleanor Jo stated with a grim look on her face.

"I know, honey, but this doesn't have anything to do with what we want or don't want. From what I've been told, the war prisoner detention camp is half-constructed already. The project should be completed soon and ready for prisoners."

"What prisoners do you think will be there?" Mama asked with a worried look on her face.

"Germans, likely," Papa said. "Rumor is, the Japanese will be placed in camps in Hearne and Huntsville. I hear-tell Japanese-Americans are even being placed in interment camps simply because of their heritage."

"What do you mean?" Mama asked.

"American citizens who look Japanese or have Japanese names are being held in camps, unable to return to their homes until the war is over."

"That's awful!" Mama began to fan herself. "I can't imagine such a thing! Those poor families! Can you imagine being kept away from your home, your friends, and your church? It doesn't seem fair!"

"There's something about a war that makes folks afraid of one another," Papa said with a sigh. "I wish it weren't true, but it is."

Eleanor Jo hated to admit it, but she was afraid of the Germans and the Japanese too. She sank down into a chair, very upset about all of the news she had just heard. "Will they hurt us? Will we be safe?"

"We will be safe," Papa assured her. "You have nothing to worry about. Though all of this does make the war seem much closer to home, doesn't it?"

Eleanor Jo and Mama both nodded, but Eleanor Jo couldn't help but wonder why the enemy soldiers would be here in Mexia. Would they stay for long? And what if Papa was wrong? What if they somehow escaped from the nearby prison camp and hurt the wonderful people in her hometown? Worse yet, what if they came here to the farm?

As she headed back outside to take a long walk in the fields, Eleanor Jo promised herself she would pray—pray for the safety of the people of Mexia and pray for the safety of her family.

Just a few weeks later, the prisoner of war (POW) camp opened. Eleanor Jo watched in fear as military jeeps drove through town, carrying German soldiers to the camp.

"I can't believe it's finally happened," she whispered to Martha Ann.

"I'm scared," her little sister said, squeezing her hand.

"Me too," Eleanor Jo admitted.

Usually when soldiers went by, she and the other girls waved. The soldiers usually waved back and then threw pieces of bubble gum, as well as their addresses. The girls always scrambled to see who could gather the most addresses, though Clydene usually won.

This time, however, Eleanor Jo didn't wave. She was too afraid of what the enemy soldiers would do. In fact, she didn't even want them to see her face, so she turned and walked in the opposite direction. She thought about writing a story in the newsletter but couldn't even bring herself to do that. For some reason, she just wanted to pretend it wasn't happening—that the enemy really hadn't come to her hometown!

Later that afternoon, her little brother James went missing.

"Help me look for him!" Mama said with a frantic look on her face. Papa searched for him in the barn, in the fields, and in the henhouse. He was nowhere to be found. Everyone scurried about, frantically searching for him. A terrible thought occurred to Eleanor Jo.

"What if..."

Perhaps one of the enemy soldiers had escaped and stolen him away. Oh, how awful that would be!

Tears flowed as she thought about it. Those mean, awful men! Had they taken her brother? Would they sweep him away, across the ocean, to live in some foreign place? Would he have to eat different foods and speak a different language? Would he be held in a prison camp, like so many others? Would she ever see him again?

Thankfully, Mama located James at last. He had fallen asleep under his bed. He had no idea others had spent the entire afternoon searching for him. And Eleanor Jo never told Mama about her fears. In fact, she didn't say anything to anyone about the prisoners of war until suppertime, when the whole family gathered around the table.

Over a warm bowl full of pinto beans, Eleanor Jo decided to tell Papa her fears. She couldn't help but cry as she talked about how afraid she had been. He assured her she had nothing to be afraid of, and he told her something rather startling.

"You need to be praying for those prisoners, Eleanor Jo."

"Praying for...the enemy?" she questioned.

"Yes, of course," Papa said. "That's what the Bible tells us to do. We are to pray for both our friends and our enemies."

That didn't make sense to Eleanor Jo until Papa explained it. "On the other side of the world, those boys have mothers, fathers, brothers, sisters, sweethearts, and friends…just like our American boys do."

Eleanor Jo's eyes grew wide. She'd never thought about that before.

"Their mothers are praying for their safety, just like your Mammy Powell prays for her son—your Uncle Welton. Their wives pray they will return home safely, just like Mary Lou prays that her new husband will return home. *All* of the fighting men are God's children—the ones we agree with and the ones we don't. Do you understand?"

"Yes." Why it had not occurred to her before, she did not know. Perhaps, she had spent so much time thinking about the Germans and Japanese as her enemies that she hadn't really thought about them as God's children. We are all part of God's creation. Why, when she thought about them that way, it seemed a little sad that God's children were quarreling and fighting. Why couldn't they just get along? Why did they have to disagree?

Then again, she and Martha Ann often bickered from time to time, didn't they?

"What will the men do while they're in the camps?" Eleanor Jo asked.

"I suppose the prisoners will do most of the things our soldiers would do," he explained. "They will get up early in the morning and eat the same type of field rations that our American boys receive. Then, I imagine many of the men will perform duties like mowing grass or hauling supplies. Others will likely be put to work as mechanics and so forth. Basically, they will be kept busy until the war ends, and then they will be returned to their families."

Eleanor Jo relaxed as she thought about all of this, but over the next few weeks, she noticed that many of the other folks in town did not seem to feel the same way her Papa did. There were plenty of stories going around about the prisoners. Some of the kids at school told wide-eyed tales about German soldiers escaping and stealing their horses and chickens, but the stories were hardly ever true.

Eleanor Jo shared with her friends at school what Papa had told her and tried her best to keep everyone calm. She also wrote an article for the newsletter. In addtion, she encouraged everyone in the Victory Club to pray for all of the soldiers—the ones fighting *for* them as well as the ones fighting *against* them. After all, it was the right thing to do.

There were all shades of lilies, multi-colored zinnias, bachelor buttons, cock's combs, and phloxes, along with Eleanor Jo's favorites, the Shasta daisies.

PLANTING SEEDS
OF FAITH

SUMMER, 1943

*T*HAT SUMMER, LIFE SEEMED TO GET BACK to normal. The school year wrapped up and the children returned to their games. They skipped rope, tossed marbles, played jacks, and swung on the tire swing which hung from a rope on the large oak tree in the yard.

Though there was plenty of time for fun, Eleanor Jo never forgot about the Victory Club or her savings bond book. She went from door to door, offering to help neighbors with all sorts of chores to earn extra nickels. She polished silver for Mrs. Urschel, a well-to-do woman in town, and dug up weeds in Mrs. Bain's garden so that she could purchase more stamps. She wrote about all of these things in her weekly newsletter, and with each passing day, she felt more and more like a journalist.

What fun it was to encourage others to join the war effort, and how Eleanor Jo loved coming up with new ideas to put in the newsletter. She encouraged others in the Victory Club to do everything they could to help out. In fact, she kept these money-making activities going all summer long. Before long, all of the children were purchasing stamps from Mama at the post office, and the whole thing became like a game.

Eleanor Jo's friend Helen came up with another terrific project idea—a Victory flower garden. The girls decided the flowers in the garden—sweet peas, zinnias, sunflowers, daisies, and so forth—would be given interesting names like trust, courage, love, and perseverance.

Helen's mother loved to work in the garden. She knew a lot about flowers, so she helped the girls. For days, they tilled an eight-foot circle, digging out the grass and loosening the soil. Then they planted the seeds and bulbs. It was a lot of work, but it was fun too. Eleanor Jo could hardly wait to see the flowers bloom.

After several days had gone by, she found herself growing anxious. She wanted the flowers to grow... quickly! Would they ever pop through the soil?

At last, the children's hard work, patience, and perseverance paid off when the flowers finally bloomed. Why, they had flowers galore! There were all shades of lilies, as well as multi-colored zinnias, bachelor buttons, cock's combs, and phloxes, along with Eleanor Jo's favorites, Shasta daisies.

Papa built the trellis on which the flowers could climb. "Tip-toe for a flight, beautiful and white," Mrs. Bain would say as she groomed the flowers to grow upward.

When the flowers were ready, members of the Victory Club plucked them up out of the ground and created colorful and fragrant bouquets. The flower bouquets were grouped into themes and given little rhymes. When the bouquets were made, the girls hand-delivered them to the families of the men serving in the armed forces.

Nearly every day, the club members would deliver bundles of flowers to some unsuspecting mother, wife, or daughter. Each time, they would explain why they had chosen that particular combination of flowers.

For instance, Eleanor Jo loved to gather the white flowers like lilies and add a dash of color to represent honesty. She would present the bouquet and sing the rhyme:

"Here is my flower, what will you do? It will grow
    honesty in me and you!
Honesty, honesty, glowing so bright. So, let's be honest
    with all our might!
My pretty flower, put in a vase. With love and care, it
    will grow grace."

Eleanor Jo loved to watch the expressions on the faces of the women as they received the flowers and listened to the rhymes.

"Oh, you've just made my day!" most would say with tears streaming down their faces.

One older woman even said, "Why, I feel like my son Johnny has brought these to me, himself!"

Eleanor Jo happened to know that Johnny was halfway across the world in the Philippines. Somehow, bringing the flowers to the families made them feel like their loved ones had returned home, if only for a moment. There was something about putting smiles on people's faces that made Eleanor Jo feel really good.

Of course, the flower garden wasn't the only garden to be tended. Mama still called upon all of the children to weed and care for the Victory vegetable garden. Many days, Eleanor Jo would crawl about on her hands and knees, picking crisp, green string beans from poles and snatching ripe red tomatoes from the vines. Mama would slice the tomatoes up and serve them at supper-time—often with ham, black-eyed peas, and cornbread. Many of the vegetables she would can, and some she would give to neighbors, especially those who were too old or frail to plant their own gardens.

One Sunday, the entire family went to church together as usual. They had a wonderful service. Eleanor Jo loved the hymn-singing best of all, especially now that Uncle

Welton had told her she had a fine voice. She sang out, not at all ashamed to be heard. Afterward, Pastor Lewis delivered a wonderful sermon about faith. Eleanor Jo listened to every word.

When the service ended, Papa invited Pastor Lewis, his wife, and their two sons over to their house for dinner. Eleanor Jo also got to invite her best friend, Clydene, as well. Eleanor Jo loved Sunday dinners best because that was the only day of the week when Mama served dessert. Eleanor Jo was excited to have company over to share the Sunday meal. Soon, they were all seated around the table, staring at big bowls of fried chicken, mashed potatoes, and okra.

Papa blessed the food, and then the feast began.

"I hear you and the other children are working very hard," Pastor Lewis said to Eleanor Jo as they ate.

She felt her cheeks turn warm as she blushed. "Yes sir."

"We're so proud of you." He flashed a warm smile. "And I hear you've turned into a writer. In fact, I've seen one of your newsletters."

"You have?" She looked at him, amazed.

"Yes, many in the community are talking about what a fine writer you are, how you will one day write for the paper and maybe even write books!"

Eleanor Jo's eyes widened at the very idea. "Oh, do you really think so?"

"Well, God gives us all special talents to be used for Him," Pastor Lewis explained. "So I've no doubt you will grow up to be quite an amazing woman of God—a great leader and a great writer!"

"All the kids at school love to read Eleanor Jo's newsletters," Clydene added.

Eleanor Jo hardly knew what to say. Had people in the community really been talking about her in such a way? Oh, how she hoped Pastor Lewis was right.

Everyone ate and ate until their tummies were quite full. At the end of the meal, Eleanor Jo looked around the table to see if every plate was empty. Mama always called empty plates "Victory plates" and reminded the children how important it was not to waste anything, not even one bite of food.

Today, Eleanor Jo happened to notice that Pastor Lewis hadn't finished his okra. Should she say something?

Thankfully, he ate the last few pieces, just as Mama proclaimed she'd made homemade banana pudding for dessert. How wonderful! Banana pudding happened to be one of Eleanor Jo's favorites!

After everyone was given a little bowl of the yummy dessert, the grown-ups began to talk about the war. Eleanor Jo found herself listening in to their conversations instead of paying attention to her food. She looked down to discover half of her banana pudding had been eaten. Startled, she turned to glance at her brother, James.

As she suspected, his spoon was mid-air, and he had bits of pudding all around his mouth. His bowl was already empty, and he'd eaten half of hers!

She started to interrupt the grown-ups to tell Mama what James had done, but decided against it when he gave her a look that seemed to say, "I'm sorry!" Instead, she offered him another bite and then finished off the rest with a smile.

In other words, she turned lemons into lemonade again. She took advantage of an opportunity to turn something bad into something good, and it made her feel mighty good too!

After the meal, the children ran off to play in the garage. This was one of their favorite places to play. The garage had tin sides and a tin roof. There was no real floor, only sand. Once inside, they decided to play church. The boys fetched several little rockers from the house so that everyone would have a place to sit or kneel. They also brought a variety of dishes.

Eleanor Jo led the singing, and Clydene acted like she was playing the piano.

"Let us all stand and sing, 'It is Well with my Soul,'" she encouraged them. The voices rang out in unison, and she didn't know when she'd ever heard such fine singing!

Pastor Lewis's youngest son, Truman, stood and faced the crowd. "I'll be the pastor!" he proclaimed. He picked up a tin dish—one with the big, bad wolf painted on it.

"I've come to you today to preach a round sermon on a square plate!" he began. Then he started to preach with great gusto. My, how that boy could preach! Why, one day he might be a real pastor, just like his father!

He started with the Bible verse from John 3:16 that Eleanor Jo loved. "*For God so loved the world,*" Truman said in his preacher-like voice, "*that he gave his only begotten Son, that whosoever believeth in him should not perish, but have everlasting life.*"

Clydene raised her hand and interrupted his sermon. "Pastor Truman," she said, "I'm sorry, but I don't know what that part about everlasting life means."

All of the children turned to gaze at Clydene in curiosity, especially Eleanor Jo. Was it possible her good friend had never asked Jesus to come and live in her heart?"

"Why, it's simply a matter of accepting Jesus Christ as your Lord and Savior, and making Him the Master of your life," Truman explained, in the very way his papa so often did. "That means He's the one in charge."

"Of everything?" Clydene's eyes grew wide.

"Yes." Truman smiled. "But once you do that, God gives you everlasting life. That means one day you get to live in heaven forever and ever."

"But, I don't know *how* to accept Jesus into my heart," Clydene responded with a shrug. "I never did it before."

"You can pray a simple prayer," Truman said. "Would you like me to help you?"

When she nodded, he closed his eyes, and Clydene listened as he prayed.

"Dear Lord, thank You for sending Your Son Jesus into the world for me."

Clydene repeated the words, but when she got to the end, she interrupted the prayer to ask, "For me? Jesus came into the world for me?"

"Yes," Truman assured her. "For you."

"And me!" Eleanor Jo added.

"And me!" all of the other children chimed in.

Truman went back to praying. "I believe that Jesus died on the cross and has saved me from my sins. I accept His gift of eternal life and ask Him to come and live in my heart. Help me to live for You, Lord!"

Clydene repeated each and every word. When she finished, all of the children shouted a joyous "Amen!"

"Now we really have something to celebrate!" Martha Ann said with a smile on her face and a happy sound in her voice. "Papa says the angels in heaven rejoice when someone comes to know the Lord. So let's pray the house down!" The children knelt down at their rockers, preparing to praise God for giving Clydene eternal life.

Just then, the garage door opened, and Papa stood there with Pastor Lewis at his side. They took one look at the children and grinned.

"Don't let us stop you!" Pastor Lewis said. "Praying is always a good idea, even in the garage."

Truman quickly explained that Clydene had just accepted Jesus, and Pastor Lewis smiled broadly. "I'm so happy," he said. "So very happy!"

He and Papa came to the front of the room and led the others in a prayer that Eleanor Jo would never forget. They prayed for Clydene first—that she would continue to live a life for the Lord. Then they prayed for the fine people of Mexia, especially those whose family members were fighting in the war. They prayed for the soldiers. And then they prayed for the prisoners of war, those men just a few miles away whose families were missing them halfway across the world.

At the end of the prayer time, there were tears in every eye. What had started out as a pretend church service had turned into a very real one, and what a wonderful one, at that!

Eleanor Jo learned a lot that summer—about resting, playing, and working. Best of all, she learned that children could really make a difference...and that made her feel just wonderful.

"V-I-C-T-O-R-Y!
Now you know the reason why!
V-I-C-T-O-R-Y!
Let us hold our banner high!"

VICTORY NIGHT!

*T*HE SUMMER WAS RAPIDLY DRAWING to a close, but Eleanor Jo and the other girls continued on with the Victory Club, even coming up with a cheer.

"V-I-C-T-O-R-Y!
Now you know the reason why!
V-I-C-T-O-R-Y!
Let us hold our banner high!"

They would march around the dairy farm, cheering in front of the cows, horses, and chickens.

All the while, Eleanor Jo thought about what Pastor Lewis had said—that she would one day be a great leader and that God had given her talents and abilities to be used for Him. Still, she longed to be as useful as she could be—right then and there!

Just a week or so before school began, Eleanor Jo came up with her best idea yet. They would host a benefit concert, inviting others in the community to a special night of entertainment in the barn. There would be a cost to attend, and people in the audience would be able to purchase lemonade and popcorn balls as well as other snacks, which Eleanor Jo hoped various merchants in town would agree to provide for free.

The club members declared it the finest idea they had ever heard of, and they began to put plans into motion at once for the most exciting Victory night celebration ever! The last Saturday evening in August would be just perfect. What a fun way to end the summer, doing something for the troops!

Papa pulled a flatbed trailer to the far end of the barn. "This will make a great stage!" he proclaimed.

Then Mama let them borrow some tablecloths and blankets from the house. "These will make nice curtains!" she explained.

"I will use flowers from the Victory flower garden to make lovely colorful bouquets," Helen announced.

One of the men from the church fixed up an old piano that had been in the barn for years, and the children rehearsed a special number for the show.

Clydene worked hard as head of the decorating committee, setting up bales of hay as seats and even putting flags and other patriotic items all around the barn. Eleanor Jo was proud to contribute the photograph she'd won of General Eisenhower, which was placed near the front. Helen and Patricia were put in charge of locating performers. They started with their own families and then asked others in the town to participate. Before long, they had a list of acts. Eleanor Jo could hardly wait!

Finally, the big night arrived. It was hot, even for August, but that didn't stop the Victory Club members from welcoming their guests. Folks paid twenty-five cents at the door and then took their seats. Before long, the whole barn was filled to overflowing. Eleanor Jo tried to count the number of people but simply couldn't. Surely there were nearly a hundred men, women, and children in attendance.

As the moment for the show to begin drew nearer, the performers grew more and more excited.

Clydene's mother was all aflutter over her upcoming solo. "I hope I do a nice job," she said. "I've had a touch of a sore throat!"

Lilly Belle Norton, a youngster who attended church with Eleanor Jo and who was to play the piano that night, came with her hair curled and pink ribbons tied on both sides. "I'm so nervous, my knees are shaking!" she proclaimed.

Joe Ray and Bobby, Clydene's brothers, were sure to be a hit. They were performing a comedy routine they had written with the help of Daddy Clyde, their father. He was such a funny man! Eleanor Jo could hardly wait to hear what they'd come up with!

Helen and her mother had written a lovely piece about the flower garden which they planned to share. Even Papa and James were happy to perform. They'd prepared a couple of fun magic tricks. Eleanor Jo, Patricia, and Clydene had written a fun little skit, which they couldn't wait to perform.

Mrs. Urschel, a well-to-do-woman from town, arrived just as they were set to go on. "I'm so sorry for my tardiness," she explained, "but I'm looking forward to reading the patriotic poem I've written just for this occasion!"

Mama rushed about with the other women, tending to the foods which folks were happy to purchase. All around the room, children and their parents nibbled on popcorn balls and drank glasses of lemonade or iced tea. Eleanor Jo watched it all in amazement. What a wonderful night this was going to be!

Mr. Holloway, Clydene's Papa, had brought his barbeque pit, and the tempting smell of barbecued spare ribs, chicken legs, and sausages filled the air. Everyone in Mexia loved Mr. Holloway's barbecue. Clydene said it was because he used a secret recipe for the sauce. Lots of folks gathered around him on this special night, spending their hard-earned nickels and dimes on the delicious food.

Soon it was time for the evening festivities to begin. Just as Pastor Lewis came forward to offer the opening prayer, an older man came in the door. He was an oil man, the richest man in town. Surely he would donate above and beyond what he had already paid.

Eleanor Jo came to the front and made introductions. She thanked everyone for coming and for their generous giving. Then it was time for the first act!

"I am so happy to introduce Mrs. Holloway, the mother of one of my best friends."

Clydene's Mama stood and approached the front of the room. Mrs. Lewis, the pastor's wife, took her place at the piano to accompany Mrs. Holloway as she sang a beautiful hymn.

Afterward, it was Mrs. Urschel's turn. Eleanor Jo couldn't help but stare at the woman's elegant dress. It was a lovely shade of blue with a white lace collar. It looked so nice with her beautiful, white hair.

"Before I begin, I would like to thank the children for putting this evening's event together," Mrs. Urschel said. "And I'm so honored to join in the festivities." She then went on to read her poem, which she had written just for that evening.

"Our brave men…so strong, so true,
Fighting a battle for me and for you;
They offer their lives in service to all,
Our heroes, they are, courageous and tall.

"By land or by sea, they give it their best,
Trusting in God to do all the rest;
And night after night, as they're dreaming of home,
They count on our prayers, so they're never alone."

When she finished, she took a hankie from her pocket and dabbed her eyes. Eleanor Jo noticed several others in the room doing the same.

Afterward, Clydene's father and brothers made the people laugh with their silly jokes and funny antics, and then Helen and her mother stood to talk about the flowers in the Victory flower garden. Eleanor Jo and her friends led everyone in the Victory chant and then performed their funny little skit. Clydene forgot her lines and Patricia got the giggles, but no one in the audience seemed to care.

One by one, the rest of the performers came forward, and Eleanor Jo introduced them to the audience. Each did a wonderful job, which made her part all the more enjoyable.

As the evening drew to a close, she introduced the one act she was most looking forward to. Mama came to the front and led the crowd in an emotional song, one they had all grown to love. They all stood and sang together…

*"Keep the Home Fires Burning, while your hearts are
    yearning,
Though your lads are far away they dream of home.
There's a silver lining through the dark clouds shining,
Turn the dark cloud inside out 'til the boys come
    home."*

When they finished, there wasn't a dry eye in the barn.

After the final performance, the people clapped and clapped. And as they left, they thanked the children for putting on such a wonderful show.

Patricia and her mother approached Eleanor Jo with smiles on their faces. "This was the most fun I've had since my sons went off to war," Mrs. Gauntt said, still smiling.

Eleanor Jo was so delighted.

After everything had been cleaned up, she yawned all the way to the house. She had just changed into her nightgown when she heard Mama gasp. She ran into the kitchen where Mama and Papa were counting the money from the evening's event.

"What is it, Mama?" Eleanor Jo asked.

"Why, I simply don't believe it!" her mother said, staring at the dollar bills and huge mound of change.

"What?"

Mama's eyes widened as she said, "We raised over two hundred dollars to send the Red Cross! Two hundred dollars!"

Eleanor Jo squealed and then clapped her hands as she jumped up and down. Before long, Martha Ann and James were in the kitchen, jumping alongside her.

They all gathered around the table, looking at the money. Then, from out of the blue, Mama started to sing. The song started softly, but within seconds, everyone had joined in and the little kitchen was filled with music.

> *"Keep the Home Fires Burning, while your hearts are*
>   *yearning,*
> *Though your lads are far away they dream of home.*
> *There's a silver lining through the dark clouds shining,*
> *Turn the dark cloud inside out 'til the boys come*
>   *home."*

Eleanor Jo closed her eyes as she sang and realized they sounded very much like a choir—a heavenly choir. In fact, she could almost hear the angels singing along.

"Oh, Mama!" Her eyes filled with tears. "He said my prayers made a difference in his life!"

THE REWARD

HE NIGHT BEFORE SCHOOL STARTED, Eleanor Jo had a hard time sleeping. She was very excited about all they had accomplished over the summer and looked forward to her seventh grade year.

The next morning, she awoke early to the sound of her Papa's voice. As always, he was singing his morning song:

"Wake up and spit on the rock. It ain't quite day, but
it's four o'clock.
I know you're tired and sleepy too, but honey, we've got
work to do!"

Eleanor Jo loved the comforting sound of his voice, and this morning she didn't even mind getting up early. She quickly ate her breakfast and then walked down to the bus stop. Minutes later, she arrived at school and greeted her friends. Together, they enjoyed the first day of the new school year.

That afternoon, as soon as she returned home, Mama had a surprise for her.

"Look what came in the mail today, Eleanor Jo," she said, handing her a letter.

"W…what is it?"

"It's from a serviceman," Mama explained. "I can tell from the address."

She looked down at the address but couldn't make much sense out of it. She ripped open the envelope and pulled out the letter with great excitement. She turned to the last page to have a look at the signature.

"Oh, Mama!" she exclaimed. "It's from George Davis, the soldier from Teague. Remember, I wrote to him last year!"

"Yes, I recall," Mama said.

They sat together at the table, and Eleanor Jo read the letter aloud.

Dear Eleanor Jo,

I'm sorry it's taken so long to write. Let me start by thanking you for your kind letter. It meant so much to hear from someone from home. Thank you for the weather update and thanks so much for bringing me up to date on all of the goings-on in Teague and Mexia.

I was thrilled to hear that the Teague High School football team is doing well. Reading about their victories made me remember my days as a boy in school. Oh, how I long for those days now! If you get the chance, please pass along a note to my best friend, Joe Matthews, and tell him that I miss him.

We've been hearing reports about all of the women at home who are working so hard, doing men's work. We are so grateful and so proud of them! My girlfriend, Kathryn Jackson, is working as the manager at a small shoe store in Teague now. Her boss is fighting on my very ship!

Now, to answer your questions—I am six foot tall and have brown, curly hair...though my hair has now been cut short. I am serving on a warship in the Pacific Ocean alongside several other Navy men from our area.

I really appreciated your story about turning lemons into lemonade. There have been so many times, especially when the war is raging around me, when it's been hard to see the good. But I keep my faith in God, and I trust He will make us victorious in battle. When that happens, I will return home, and perhaps we can all share a nice cold pitcher of lemonade! I look forward to that day.

And now, for the sad news...the reason it took me so long to write is that I've been in the hospital since early summer. I was injured in battle at that time. For a while, the doctors thought my leg was a goner, but it has healed nicely. I know it has, at least in part, because of your prayers. I'm so grateful—you will never know how much. All of our fighting men need those prayers, so keep them coming!

In closing, I would like to share a Bible verse that has meant a lot to me since boarding the ship. It's found in 2 Chronicles 15:7, and reads, "Be ye strong therefore, and let not your hands be weak: for your work shall be rewarded." I say those words aloud every day so that I never forget to keep on keeping on. You do the same, and your work will be rewarded.

Thank you again for your letter and your prayers. Until we meet in person...keep the home fires burning!

Private George Davis

P.S. V for Victory!

Eleanor Jo's hands were trembling as she gripped the letter in her hand. "Oh, Mama!" Her eyes filled with tears. "He said my prayers made a difference in his life!"

"Prayers always make a difference, honey," her mother said with a nod.

Eleanor Jo wiped away a tear. "It makes me feel so good to know my hard work is paying off. And all of the things the members of the Victory Club have done—the scrap drive, the fundraisers—it's all been worth it, just to read his words!"

"Your hard work has paid off, to be sure."

Eleanor Jo glanced back down at the letter one last time and then looked up with a smile. "And how wonderful to know that his favorite scripture is ours, as well!"

"That is no coincidence, I am sure," Mama agreed. "Surely that is the Lord's doing."

Eleanor Jo thought about the soldier's words for the rest of the day. She thought about them as she went about her chores in the barn, and she thought about them as she set the table for supper. She thought about them as she climbed into bed for a good night's sleep.

In fact, Eleanor Jo thought about the young soldier's words from that day on. She would be strong and courageous. She wouldn't give up…no matter what!

Many times over the following months, she would lift her hand to the sky, giving the Victory sign. "V for Victory!" she would cry out. "V for Victory!" With the Lord's help, they would surely win this war—and all of their fighting men would return home to celebrate together.

Until then, she would keep on keeping on, working hard at home, at school, and with the Victory Club, doing everything the Lord called her to do—and her hard work would be rewarded. Of that, she was quite sure.

"I really do come from a long line of hard workers," Rachel Ann said with a smile.

Epilogue

WISH IT, WATCH IT, *MAKE* IT!

*R*ACHEL ANN LISTENED TO THE END OF her grandmother's story and then stared out at the dairy farm in awe. To think, a war halfway across the world had come here—to the tiny town of Mexia, where Grand Doll once lived.

"I've heard of World War II before, but I never realized it affected so many people right here in your hometown," Rachel Ann said. "It's hard to believe all of those things happened right here in Texas."

"Imagine living through it at your age!" Grand Doll said. "We had never experienced any of those things before. War, rationing, prison camps, scrap drives—they were all new to us."

"It sounds like you enjoyed joining in the war effort," Rachel Ann said.

"Oh, I did. I can't tell you how much I enjoyed helping out. Writing letters to the servicemen was my favorite part. That's something I will never forget, and it's a legacy

I hope to pass on to my children and grandchildren—a love for the men and women who serve in the armed forces."

"May I ask you a question?" Rachel Ann asked after a minute.

"Sure, honey," Grand Doll said.

"What ever happened to your cousin David Martin and to Uncle Welton?"

"Ah. David Martin served in the armed forces and arrived home, healthy, and strong, thanks to Aunt Vera's prayers. And Uncle Welton..." A smile lit her face as she spoke. "After the war ended, Uncle Welton fell in love with a wonderful woman named Helen. She had been captured by the Germans and lived as a prisoner of war overseas."

"Really?"

"Yes, it's true. She survived and was returned to the United States where she met my Uncle Welton. They married and traveled all over the world."

"Wow." Rachel Ann shook her head. "Sounds like the people in our family were made of tough stuff."

"Like my papa used to say, 'Tough times call for tough people,'" Grand Doll reminded her. "And there's no time like war time to find out just how tough a person can be. That's how it was when our soldiers were fighting in the Pacific and in Europe. But in the middle of it, those of us who remained at home learned *so* many lessons—especially about working hard."

"I do know what it means to work hard," Rachel Ann said.

"Yes, and that's why I told you that story," Grand Doll explained. She gave Rachel Ann a sweet smile. "Don't you see, honey? You make wonderful grades. You lead your basketball team to victory, and you work in school clubs and keep up your chores. I understand, because I was the same way as a girl."

"You started the Victory Club!"

"Yes, and it was wonderful, but it was a lot of work. So I know what you're going through. I can see how tired you get, and I know you must feel like giving up sometimes."

Rachel Ann giggled. "Mostly in the mornings when it's time to 'wake up and spit on the rock,' as your Papa would say."

They both laughed.

"My papa certainly new the value of working hard." Grand Doll looked back out over the land. "He kept this farm going when others across the country gave up. We had plenty of milk and food. We never did without. And my Mama…" A dreamy look came into her eyes. "My Mama was the hardest working woman I ever knew. She didn't build ships or manage a store, but she kept the cleanest house in town and cooked up a storm. She also worked part-time as the postmistress."

"I really do come from a long line of hard workers," Rachel Ann said with a smile.

"That's why I love that scripture so much," Grand Doll said, "the one my mama and my papa taught me—*Be ye strong therefore, and let not your hands be weak: for your work shall be rewarded.* There's a newer version that reads, *But as for you, be strong and do not give up, for your work will be rewarded.* I like to say, 'You can wish it to happen, watch it happen, or you can make it happen.'"

"I like that!" Rachel Ann said. "I'm the kind of person who likes to make things happen."

"I know you are," Grand Doll said, and she gave her a wink. "You're a lot like me in that way, for sure."

"Maybe I can start a Victory Club at my school," Rachel Ann suggested.

"Sounds like a good idea," her grandmother said, "and I'll be happy to help."

A dozen ideas went through Rachel Ann's mind as she thought about the possibilities for what they could do. Just then, she thought about Grand Doll's story again. "How old were you when the war ended?" she asked.

Grand Doll wrinkled her brow as she thought. "The war ended in 1945 when the Allied forces won against the Germans and the Japanese. I was fourteen years old, just your age."

"It seems kind of strange," Rachel Ann said. "The United States is now friends with Japan and with Germany. What happened?"

"Time," Grand Doll said. "Time has healed many of those old wounds. Even broken relationships can be mended with hard work."

"I just wish there was no such thing as war," Rachel Ann said with a sigh. "It seems like every time I turn on the television, someone is talking about a war someplace around the world."

"People will always fight for what they believe is right," Grand Doll explained. "That's just what our brave men and women in the armed forces did during the Second World War, and that's just what they're doing now all over the world. The legacy of bravery and hard work goes on."

With misty eyes, Grand Doll gave the dairy farm one last look before asking if Rachel Ann was ready to head home. Rachel Ann said yes but turned back to look at the home where Grand Doll had grown up. She closed her eyes and could almost hear the sound of children's voices raised in a victory chant.

Just for fun, Rachel Ann lifted her hand to the air, forming a "V" with her fingers, and shouted the words, "V for Victory!" Somehow, just saying them made her think she could accomplish anything—with God's help.

Fun Facts
and More

§ President Roosevelt called December 7, 1941, "a day that will live in infamy." Today, we remember that date as the anniversary of the bombing of Pearl Harbor. Over three thousand American servicemen were killed during the attack on Pearl Harbor.

§ During WWII, the nations of the world were divided into two basic categories. The "Axis" powers included the countries of Germany, Italy, and Japan. The "Allied" powers were basically all of the countries that opposed the Axis powers, such as the U.S., Great Britain, and Russia.

§ During his dictatorship, Adolph Hitler and his followers were responsible for the deaths of over six million Jews, as well as millions of other civilians and servicemen. Hitler's Reign of Terror would have likely gone on much longer if not for the Allied involvement in the war.

§ The word "victory" was very popular during WWII. There were Victory gardens and even Victory plates.

§ Families during WWII were allotted rationing stamps to purchase shoes, sugar, and many other items.

§ To show their appreciation, people around the country wrote letters to servicemen during WWII. These letters lifted the spirits of the servicemen.

§ There were over six hundred Prisoner of War Camps in the U.S. during WWII. Many of the prisoners lived under better living conditions in these camps than they would have in their own military camps.

§ During WWII, many Japanese-Americans (American citizens) were forced to leave their homes and live in internment camps simply because they were part Japanese.

§ V–E day (Victory in Europe day) took place on May 7/8, 1945. V–J day (Victory in Japan day) took place on August 15, 1945.

§ During WWII, women took over men's jobs. Over six million women joined the workforce. For the first time ever, women became store managers and held other such positions. "Rosie the Riveter" became a popular name for working women.

§ The song "Keep the Home Fires Burning" was written by Lena Ford in 1914 during the First World War.

§ Do you pray for our president and other political leaders? Can you think of three good reasons why you should?

§ Do you know anyone in the armed services? If so, do you pray for him or her, and for the rest of America's fighting men and women? (They need and appreciate your prayers.)

§ Have you ever written a letter to a serviceman or woman? (If not, why not ask your parents or teacher for more information on how you can do that?)

§ On December 7, 1941, everything changed for America in one day. Have you ever had a day when you got some news that changed your life?

§ Is there any mention of wars in the Bible? If so, what does the Word of God have to say about fighting for what is right?

§ What do you supposed eventually happened to all of the German and Japanese prisoners of war?

§ Why is it important to work hard and not give up? What does the Bible say about laziness?

§ What does the word "victory" mean to you? Have you celebrated any victories lately?

§ Have you ever had to make lemonade out of lemons like Eleanor Jo did in this story?

§ Back in the 1940s, women were working in men's jobs for the first time ever. Nowadays, a lot of women have jobs. Name a few of the women you know who work jobs (in the home or outside the home).

*Be ye strong therefore, and let not your hands be
weak; for your work shall be rewarded.*
—*2 Chronicles 15:7*

This verse urges us to be strong and to work hard. It
also promises us that we will be rewarded for our hard
work.

It has been said, "Hard work never hurt anyone."
This statement is true in the physical realm and in our
spiritual lives as well. As Christians, we are called upon
to work hard physically so that our needs will be met
and to work hard spiritually for the good of others. In
1 Thessalonians 4:11, Paul is writing to his friends and
the church in Thessalonica, encouraging them and
commending them for their love for one another and
their hard work for the Lord. Paul tells them, *Aspire to
lead a quiet life, to mind your own business, and to work
with your own hands, as we commanded you* (NKJV).

Paul talks about working hard many times in the
scriptures because hard work is of great importance and

value. In 2 Thessalonians 3:6–12 (NKJV), we find Paul urging the church to work hard and not to be idle:

But we command you, brethren, in the name of our Lord Jesus Christ, that you withdraw from every brother who walks disorderly and not according to the tradition which he received from us. For you yourselves know how you ought to follow us, for we were not disorderly among you; nor did we eat anyone's bread free of charge, but worked with labor and toil night and day, that we might not be a burden to any of you, not because we do not have authority, but to make ourselves an example of how you should follow us. For even we were with you we commanded you this: If anyone will not work, neither shall he eat. For we hear that there are some who walk among you in a disorderly manner, not working at all, but are busybodies. Now those who are such we command and exhort through our Lord Jesus Christ that they work in quietness and eat their own bread.

In this passage of scripture, Paul is very serious in his command to work hard. He goes so far as to say that "if you do not work, you do not eat." Another famous person in history also made this statement. Do you know who the person was? It was John Smith. When Jamestown, Virginia was founded in 1608, and John Smith was elected president of the local council, he instituted the following law: *He who does not work, will not eat.*

Paul is also concerned about people being idle. *To be idle* means "to do nothing." When people are idle, they seem to get into trouble. Paul is urging us to work hard, to stay busy, and not only to accomplish the task at hand, but also to keep our eye on the goal so that we will be rewarded.

In this book, we find Eleanor Jo working hard on the farm, at school, and with her Victory Club. The story takes place in the 1940s during World War II.

This period in history was a time of great upheaval in our country. Farmers were called upon to contribute their labors by donating much of their harvest to the nation. People everywhere were asked to ration (to use sparingly) many items such as sugar and milk so that these could be used for the men fighting in the war. Giving food, clothing, blankets, and other items to the military was a part of what was known as the "war effort." During these years, friends and neighbors needed to stand together, especially in prayer, and to work hard for the good of all.

How have you contributed to your family and others by working hard?

_____

_____

_____

_____

Do you have daily chores assigned to you?

_____

_____

_____

_____

What are some of the things you do that are out of the ordinary? Do you ever do something that you haven't been told to do just because you want to bless someone like your mom, dad, grandparent, brother, or sister? In Matthew 5:41, Jesus said, "*And whoever compels* [commands or orders] *you to go one mile, go with him two*" (NKJV). That means we should always be looking for opportunities to bless others.

Philippians 2:13–15 says, *For it is God who works in you both to will and to do for His good pleasure. Do all things without complaining* [grumbling] *and disputing* [arguing or debating], *that you may be blameless and harmless, children of God without fault in the midst of a crooked and perverse generation, among whom you shine as lights in the world* (NKJV).

According to this verse, when we work without complaining, we are blameless and we shine as lights for the entire world to see. Isn't that a neat way to be a witness for God and to be a blessing to others?

Are you quick to work and to help out?

_____

_____

Do you work without complaining?

_____

_____

Give some examples from your own life of how you help others and work hard without complaining.

_____

_____

_____

_____

_____

_____

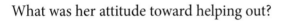

Now give some examples of how Eleanor Jo's work on the farm would benefit her family and ultimately contribute to those fighting in the war.

_____

_____

_____

_____

_____

What was her attitude toward helping out?

_____

_____

_____

_____

_____

What was the name of the club she formed? What were some of the club members' specific projects?

_____

_____

_____

_____

Eleanor Jo also organized a fundraiser. What was the name of the organization that benefited from this fundraiser?

_____

_____

Have you ever volunteered to work for the benefit of a particular charity or your school or church? If so, explain.

_____

_____

_____

_____

In Proverbs 31, we read about a virtuous woman who is always working with her hands—serving her family, God, and others. We are not to be concerned only with ourselves, but with God and others too. When we work and serve others, and pray and praise God as well, we can be called "a woman of virtue."

Are you willingly extending your hands to God in prayer for someone else? Sometimes working hard with our hands in prayer is one of the most difficult tasks but also one of the most rewarding. Give some examples of how you have helped others through prayer.

_____

_____

_____

_____

_____

_____

_____

_____

_____

Do you know what the word is that describes praying to God on behalf of someone else? Ask your parent, grandparent, or guardian if you need help finding the word.

_____

Also give examples of how you have helped others by ministering to or serving them; for example, you could tell how you helped an elderly neighbor with her yard or about a visit you made to a nursing home.

_____
_____
_____
_____
_____
_____
_____
_____

Forming a Victory Club is a great idea for your school, church, neighborhood, or friends. Victory Clubs bring people together to work toward a common goal and forge relationships that will last a lifetime. Why not think about starting a Victory Club and organizing some outreaches for your community? This type of organization instills an "other's oriented" mindset and a "working hard" mentality!

§ Decide where the organization should be held: school, church, neighborhood, or home

§ Decide how often to hold meetings: weekly or bimonthly

§ Recruit members: classmates, friends, neighbors, or church members

§ Elect officers:

- President (president presides over meetings and helps in making decisions)
- Secretary (secretary records the minutes of the meetings)
- Treasurer (treasurer is in charge of keeping track of the money)
- Project Leaders (each project leader is in charge certain projects)
- Refreshment Leader (refreshment leader is in charge of organizing refreshments)
- Chaplain (chaplain is in charge of Bible reading and organizing the Bible study)

§ Come up with your own Victory chant, motto, or song

§ Write Victory letters to the men and women in the
United States Armed Forces

§ Plant a Victory vegetable garden:
- Find a good location for your garden
- Research to find out the best types of vegetables to
plant according to the season and climate
- Work together as a team to raise the best vegeta-
bles possible
- Harvest the vegetables and then wash and prepare
them to give away
- Bag the vegetables in extra grocery bags you have
at your home
- Distribute the vegetables to elderly neighbors,
church or local food pantries, or families in need

§ Plant a Victory flower garden:
- Research the best flowers to plant in your climate
or geographical region
- Have each club member plant a flower garden in
his or her yard, if possible

- Water and feed your flowers according to the instructions given by your local nursery or garden center, or by following the directions on the container or package
- Cut the flowers when they are in full bloom
- Prepare the cut flowers to give away by:
  - Arranging flowers in an inexpensive vase found at a garage sale (Be sure to put enough water in the vase to cover the ends of the stems; remind the recipient to fill the vase with water.)
  - Wrapping the bottom part of stems in several wet paper towels and covering with foil to seal (For a special touch, wrap tissue paper [white or colored] around the covered stem; tie on a pretty ribbon, and the flowers are ready to give away.)
- Give the flowers to nursing home residents, elderly neighbors, or single mothers

§ Hold a Victory fundraiser. There are many worthy organizations that you can raise money for, including your church body, the American Red Cross, the Salvation Army, or even your own club so that you can have money to do the things you want to do. Here are some ideas for fundraisers:
- Organize a garage sale; have every member contribute items for the sale

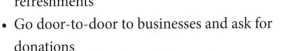

- Put on a show and charge for tickets and refreshments
- Go door-to-door to businesses and ask for donations
- Make some craft items and sell them to neighbors, relatives, or local churches
- Have a lemonade stand and sell baked goods as well

§ Hold Victory prayer meetings and intercede for:
- Our country, the president, the legislative branch, and the judicial branch
- The United States Armed Forces
- Churches all over America
- The needs of the members of your club and their families and neighbors

§ Conserve and recycle by:
- Cutting back on electricity
- Cutting back on water
- Recycling plastic, glass, and paper
- Taking recyclables to a recycling plant

Victory Club Meeting
Order of Business

§ Open meeting with prayer
§ Recite the Pledge of Allegiance
§ Have Bible reading and Bible study
§ Review previous meeting's minutes
§ Discuss ongoing projects
§ Work on projects in progress
§ Outline new projects
§ Have a time of sharing
§ Have refreshments

The Eleanor Series

ELEANOR CLARK CONCEIVED THE IDEA for *The Eleanor Series* while researching her family's rich American history. Motivated by her family lineage, which had been traced back to the early 17th century, a God-ordained idea emerged: the legacy left by her ancestors provided the perfect tool to reach today's children with the timeless truths of patriotism, godly character, and miracles of faith. Through her own family's stories, she instills in children a love of God and country, along with a passion for history. With that in mind, she set out to craft this collection of novels for the youth of today. Each story in *The Eleanor Series* focuses on a particular character trait and is laced with the pioneering spirit of one of Eleanor's true-to-life family members. These captivating stories span generations, are historically accurate, and highlight the nation's Christian heritage of faith. Twenty-first century readers—both children and parents—are sure to relate to these amazing character-building stories of young Americans while learning Christian values and American history.

LOOK FOR ALL OF THESE BOOKS
IN THE ELEANOR SERIES:

Christmas Book—*Eleanor Jo: A Christmas to Remember*
ISBN-10: 0-9753036-6-X
ISBN-13: 978-0-9753036-6-5

Available in 2007

Book One—*Mary Elizabeth: Welcome to America*
ISBN-10: 0-9753036-7-8
ISBN-13: 978-0-9753036-7-2

Book Two—*Victoria Grace: Courageous Patriot*
ISBN-10: 0-9753036-8-6
ISBN-13: 978-0-9753036-8-9

Book Three—*Katie Sue: Heading West*
ISBN-10: 0-9788726-0-6
ISBN-13: 978-0-9788726-0-1

Book Four—*Sarah Jane: Liberty's Torch*
ISBN-10: 0-9753036-9-4
ISBN-13: 978-0-9753036-9-6

Book Five—*Eleanor Jo: The Farmer's Daughter*
ISBN-10: 0-9788726-1-4
ISBN-13: 978-0-9788726-1-8

Book Six—*Melanie Ann: A Legacy of Love*
ISBN-10: 0-9788726-2-2
ISBN-13: 978-0-9788726-2-5

Visit our Web site at: www.eleanorseries.com

About the Author

LEANOR CLARK LIVES in central Texas with Lee, her husband of over 50 years, and as matriarch of the family, she is devoted to her 5 children, 17 grandchildren, and 5 great grandchildren.

Born the daughter of a Texas sharecropper and raised in the Great Depression, Eleanor was a female pioneer in crossing economic, gender, educational, and corporate barriers. An executive for one of America's most prestigious ministries, Eleanor later founded her own highly successful consulting firm. Her appreciation of her American and Christian heritage comes to life along with her exciting and colorful family history in the youth fiction series *The Eleanor Series*.